WATEHICA Book II

Stories of the Hunkpapa Band of the Great Sioux Native

Eya Mani

Trafford rev. 07/21/2021

North America & international
toll-free: 844-688-6899 (USA & Canada)
fax: 812 355 4082

STANDING ROCK SIOUX TRIBE

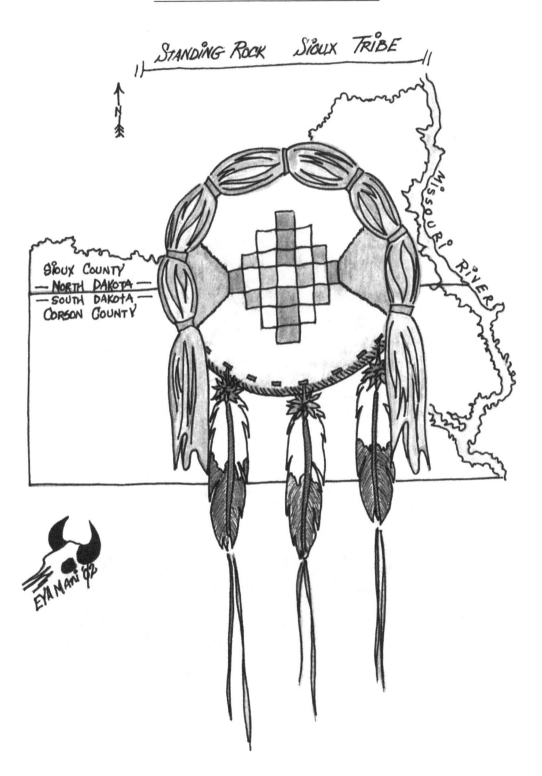

ABOUT THE AUTHOR...

The author lives on the Standing Rock Reservation in South Dakota with his wife, his children and his grandchildren. Both John Luke and his wife Sandra are full blood Hunkpapa Lakota...

Born in July of 1949, he was raised by his grandparents, and later his aunts and uncles took this responsibility. Since his extended family knew only the Lakota way of life, his upbringing and writings reflect those beliefs and customs.

John Luke is a musician, a cowboy, an artist, tipi maker, councilman, poet, writer and storyteller. And as a public speaker, John Luke has also hosted his own radio talk show titled, 'Ideas, Hopes, and Dreams...Inc.' which addressed veterans issues...

Having driven the United States as a long haul truck driver, John Luke is also proud to be a United States Marine and a combat veteran of Vietnam...

He took his pen name 'Eya Mani' in 1995, when he entered his first poem, Circle, in a contest and won. In 1999 he was designated 'Poet Laureate' for his work on Smartgirl, and in 2000, his work was used to produce the video commemorating Veterans Day by television station WB2, out of Denver, Colorado... which was broadcast worldwide.

John Luke took his grandfather's name, Eya Mani or Speaks Walking, to honor his maternal grandfather, John Luke Speaks Walking, and the work he did for the community of Rock Creek...and the people of Standing Rock.

"WATEHICA...That Which You Hold Dear..." Book I is a small collection of poems and short stories...

"WATEHICA... That Which You Hold Dear..." Book II is a larger collection of poems and short stories ...both books are filled with historical, cultural, and humorous stories, some very old, some contemporary...

Eya Mani's forth coming novel, "IYO'HI...the Journey" is a chronicle of events the Lakota of his band experienced to be where they are today...physically ...spiritually...and socially. The record is kept much as the Lakota winter count ...where only one or two events are recorded on the buffalo hide, telling of the band's history for that year...

You are invited, to come...and take the Journey...

John Luke Flyinghorse Sr. will be your guide ...you will not be disappointed.

Hau!

10 SHORT STORIES BY EYA MANI
OCTOBER 2011

ZEZECA

From the Author

Zezeca (Snake) was written in Spearfish, SD in February of 2000.

It is intended merely as a learning tool, and to make people think of all the outside influences that fashion and shape our lives, whether real or imagined.

In our story overwhelming poverty, unemployment, and hunger forced our main character to act rashly, but forgivably so.

If our main character would have taken the other option he had been thinking about, the story would have ended and we would be left without anything to think about.

And so is Lakota storytelling.

We must leave the listeners something which they can take with them from our storytelling circle.

As I make my new home here, in a new land, in a new town, and in a new millennium, I look forward to meeting new people and forging new friendships. I hope that the Spirit that brought me here will allow me to create and write in the manner the old ones would approve.

Lakota stories must be told and that without prejudice or consequence.

I give thanks to Wakan Tanka daily for the blessing that he has allowed me, to create and to share.

I pray that I would always remain worthy of these gifts...

And now I offer you "ZEZECA".

Hau!
(for my nephew JB)

ZEZECA

A Short Story
by
Eya Mani

The man had been standing on the south rim of the hill overlooking the Hump Creek, which lay below to the north.

It had taken him many hours to reach this point in his hunt for food, and now he stood looking down at the weapons that lay on the ground at his feet.

He had counted and recounted the ammunition he carried for each of the three weapons he had brought with him.

And again he took the K-bar from its scabbard and he checked the blades sharpness.

Earlier, that morning he had spent hours honing the blade to a razors edge while he planned out the day's hunt.

This was the last place he was going to cover in his search for wild game.

He was out about 15 miles west from his home in Rock Creek on the Standing Rock Sioux Indian Reservation in South Dakota.

He sat down and rolled a smoke, took a farmer's match from his shirt pocket, swiped it on his thread bare blue jeans, and lit it as his eyes surveyed his intended avenue of approach.

He knew full well that there would be no food on the table for his family that night and he ached inside because he loved his new wife and family so much.

He ground out his cigarette in the dry powder fine earth, hung his head and wept again, but again, no tears came.

He knew what he had to do.

The choices were not many.

He picked up the 30.06 rifle he had brought for big game, threw a round into the chamber and wiped at his eyes.

As he sat thinking about the difficulties he was encountering in his life, his thoughts came around to his journey to where he now sat and he noticed something strange.

Since his arrival to this vantage point unseen and even as he made his way here, he had not seen or heard any birds that used to shrill and whistle at him as he went past their territories and their nesting places. Today there was none of that, and come to think of it there were no insects or insect sounds that he could recall either.

This was indeed very strange.

Back home in Rock Creek, the young mother and her three hungry children awaited the return of their father who they hoped would be successful this time. But she also knew that there would be no meat on the table that night because there was no wild game in that part of the country any longer.

The drought had seen to that.

The young woman's husband was a fine young man, recently discharged from the Marines.

She remembered how handsome and proud he wore his dress blue uniform with the red NCO stripe running down the side of his blue dress pants.

He had pride and integrity and he was proud of his family. But times were bad and the rivers and creeks had long since dried up leaving only large muddy ponds that were now home to the trapped fish that were not fortunate enough to escape the drought.

And the wild game either simply left the country or had died of starvation or thirst much like the livestock that were being sold off in record numbers by the area ranchers, many of whom were leasing the family lands.

The time was the mid 1950's and everyone would remember this as one of the worst of times, if they survived long enough to retell their stories.

During the young hunter's absence, events had occurred that brought joy to his wife and family back home.

It seems a young female cow had been trying to reach some moisture from a culvert on the road leading to her grandmother's home and it had gotten its head caught in the culvert and had broken its neck, trying to escape.

Because the heifer was still alive, the rancher had bled the animal and had brought it to her grandmother's home for butchering.

The hunter rolled another smoke and sat quietly thinking, weighing the outcome of his decision. He knew he would hurt his family either way, but his pride and honor would not let him change his mind.

He had not taken any food at home for two days now.

He let his children eat his share, but instead of making him feel better about his sacrifices, he was feeling all the more hopeless in his endeavors to at least keep his family fed.

There was no work of any sort on the reservation, nor for that matter, in the small reservation towns around the reservation. The jobs that were to be had were given to the non-Lakota, but he didn't blame anyone for their choices, he had his own to make, and now he had made his and he hoped that no one would blame him either.

He thought about his wife most of all.

She had stood by him no matter what and in these hard times when she was playful and she would bring up happier times that they'd shared he knew she was going to miss him most of all.

He was now feeling the effects of his fast and the hot dry August heat did not help at all.

On his trek out here his vision was becoming blurred, his sweat had stopped and now to add to his misery, he was starting to get a headache.

He also had a very great thirst and he decided he would look for water later, perhaps in one of the many creeks below. Besides, after what he was going through, drinking polluted water could not be the worst thing that he could do or that could happen to him.

Maybe he would find enough water to replace that which he lost...perhaps.

Anyways he might as well get on with it.

As he was getting to his feet, he thought he had seen movement on one of the many trails below.

His Marine Corps training took over and he ducked down and sat back, trying to make himself as small an intruder as he could.

He hoped if there was anything there, he had not been seen or noticed.

Then rising up on his knees, just enough to peer over the hilltop through the grass, he surveyed the creeks and draws leading from the hill where he now sat, down to the creek below, but there was nothing!

He wiped his eyes again, trying to clear them so he could make sure of what he had seen, then he rose and peered over the hill through the grass again, and there it was!

His mind raced!

Whatever it was, it was coming up the draw directly toward him, but it was approaching at a snails pace.

He hunkered back down and he tried to think if he had ever seen anything like this.

Slowly, he rose to his knees just enough to look through the dry grass to observe what ever it was that was making its way slowly up the hill towards him.

It seemed to be following the cow path along the bottom of the draw he had intended to cover first.

Licking his lips, he rose slowly to his knees and again and he peered through the grass and his mind raced!

Wait!

Just wait a minute there!

He had heard all the old stories of such things, but he never really believed in them.

Well, maybe only as entertainment.

Stories were sometimes told to keep the young ones interested when things in camp slowed and they became restless.

Now he wasn't so sure...

The old ones used to tell tales of large animals and beasts that come out of the earth during bad times such as these, and the absence of game and drought was attributed to their presence.

Whether the wild game had fled the country for fear of them or whether they had indeed been devoured by these creatures is unknown, yet here one was. And he was going to meet it face to face and if he survived, he would know first hand.

If he survived!

Again he leaned forward and kneeling, he peered through the grass.

This time he watched it a bit longer before he settled back down to think about this.

This creature was unlike any he had ever seen heard or read about.

It appeared to be as high as a large dog and through the shimmering heat, he thought that at times it appeared to be transparent because he was able to see through portions of it, yet other parts of it were always visible!

What on earth!

As he watched, at times the creature would stop its forward motion, and it appeared to raise its head and test the winds, as if searching for a scent.

This worried him because although the air was almost still and the heat was stifling, an occasional breeze from the south would gently brush his skin. And he knew that the air would gently carry his scent down to what ever this thing was, and the fight would be on!

All this had taken place in but a few minutes, but now as he watched, his fears were realized.

It had obviously detected him and it was now on the move and definitely headed his way!

The thought of him becoming its next meal frightened him, for he surely couldn't kill it, at least not with the weapons he had at hand, it was much too large.

Now, on its journey up the hill toward him, the beast seemed to drop out of sight, so he crawled towards the edge of the hilltop to get a better look.

When he realized he was the creatures intended next meal, he quickly rose to his feet and gathered the weapons, loading each to capacity.

After he made sure his K-bar was easily at hand, he walked to the edge and looked down the steep hill at his approaching foe.

Then he knew!

This was a giant snake!

Probably the same one he had heard about in the camp fire stories, the one they say that nothing could escape it because of its size and speed.

Knowing the speed normal size snakes could attain, he knew he had little time.

He would not make a stand, instead he would take the fight to this new enemy as best he could, because he knew this monster snake would run him down in no time flat.

From his vantage point, he had a clear view and field of fire toward his approaching enemy.

As the huge snake came charging up the hill, he could clearly see its muscles moving under its skin, bringing the monster closer and closer at an alarming rate!

He quickly lay the larger caliber weapon down, and in the kneeling position and with precision shots, he emptied the 17 rounds from the .22 rifle into the creature's head.

Thinking "this should at least slow the damn thing down", but the huge snake seemed to shake off the gun fire and it hesitated for just a second.

Then, with renewed vigor and with increased speed, it continued its charge up the hill.

He could not tell if he had done any damage, but he slung the empty .22 rifle over his shoulder, then he picked up the 30.06 next and took careful aim.

His adrenaline was flowing and his vision had cleared, and he knew exactly what he must do if he were to survive.

He again emptied his weapon into the head of the advancing creature, making sure his shots were centered between the creature's eyes.

But he had no way of knowing if his shots were doing any damage, this creature didn't appear to bleed!

If he was to live, then he must do something, and he must do it now!

Slinging the 30.06 over his back, he picked up the 12 gauge shotgun and threw a round into the chamber.

The shotgun held only 5 rounds, but he knew it would probably give him enough time to get past this creature, buy him some time, but either way, it was now or never!

With his renewed strength, the keenness of his vision and the clarity of his thought returned.

He knew he didn't want to die this way.

Never to be found, seen or heard from again.

He would just be another "missing person" that everyone would talk about and the rumors would abound.

Then eventually, someone would find his weapons and expended shell casings and then everyone would again make up stories of what had happened to him and he knew he didn't want to die this way.

He undid the snap holding his K-bar in place.

Now he was ready!

Taking a deep breath, he let out an extended shout as he raced headlong down the hill, directly toward the advancing beast.

He continued shouting as he ran, and he waited until he was within a few feet of the still approaching monster when he fired his first shot, laying open a flap of skin but still he could see no blood.

The first blast from the shotgun stopped the monster this time, but whether from confusion or from the punishment he was meting out, he did not know and he did not care.

He jacked another round into the chamber and fired into the animal, peeling back the skin exposing bone but still he saw no blood.

Still shouting, he raced right past the monster, firing as he ran, emptying his shotgun into the body of the creature as he flew by. Each shot opening up the creature's skin, exposing torn and shredded muscles and with his last shot he drew blood.

He could see that his shots had indeed hurt this creature, "Good! I just might get out of this alive," he thought as he raced on down the hill and across the creek.

Three days had passed when he came to his senses.

He was at home, sitting in a chair at his own table, with a good hot meal set before him, but he was not hungry.

His wife had prepared a wonderful meal for him and she was trying to coax him into eating.

They say that he had been brought home by one of the neighbors who happened to be coming home from town that evening.

They say they had found him running on the road, and when they stopped to ask him where he was going, he just got into the back of their truck without saying a word.

When the neighbors were asked about his weapons, they said he had no rifles or ammunition and the scabbard for his K-bar was empty as well.

They also say the young man got up from the table without a word and he walked to the river and jumped into one of the mud puddles that the Grand River had become, with all his clothes on, and he just sat there.

After a couple of hours of sitting in the big mud puddle that was the river, he returned home, took a bath and changed his clothes.

Finally he did eat but all the while, he never said a word to anyone about what had happened to him.

When the young man finally broke his silence, four days had passed since his return.

It was the evening of the fourth day, when the men were gathered around the shade visiting and telling stories, when the young man came into the circle.

He told what had happened to him.

He spoke of his fear and what he had felt, and what he had done, and when he was finished telling, he got up and went home and went to bed.

The men sitting around the shade didn't have any more stories to tell, they just rolled smokes and thought about what they had just heard, and they knew what they had to do.

The young man with the beautiful young wife, rose early the next day, put on his best clothing, kissed his wife who was still asleep, and he walked out of the village.

About the same time that same morning, the men saddled their best horses and they too left, riding west.

They were all armed and at day break, three hours later they sat on their horses overlooking the breaks where the young man had first seen this monster snake.

They sat rolling smokes looking down the hill into the darkness.

As they waited for the sun to come up, the sunlight slowly revealed the carnage and the men knew exactly what had happened, but none would say a word about it.

They just knew.

"Geez, that's too bad...ennit?" one of the old cowboys finally said after a very long silence.

"You know, I didn't think that they would ever come out this far?"

"Guess they must have been foraging."

Then after another very long silence, "They say they only come out around the Missouri, and it's usually at times like these, but I guess you just never can know."

The riders had been letting their horses catch their breath after the exertion of a long steady gait on their way out here, and only the old cowboy had spoken.

As they turned their horses to leave he spoke again, "yep, it's just too bad."

Below them in the cow path running parallel along the draw leading up the hill, lay eight dead pigs.

Indeed a slaughter had occurred here.

But the young man would never know.

He would never return to the village alive again.

And neither would his wife and children ever hear from him or see him again.

He just would never know!

Hau!
(for JB)

THE DEER HUNTER

From the Author

In 1992 I was on my way to Denver, Colorado with my father-in-law and one of our friends.

The time was fall and it was raining... the trip was going to be long.

We started out late in the evening so we could be in Denver the next morning. We had driven about halfway and we had been riding mostly in silence. We must have all been thinking about the same things because one by one we started telling stories we had heard.

Some were silly stories we told to pass the time.

The Deer Hunter is such a story.

Of course the story was told in the Lakota Language and this made the story all the more funny.

When the language is translated, sometimes some of the meaning is lost. I think I have captured the humorous intent of the story and that is what I wish to share with you, the Lakota humor.

We see humor in everything, it is our way of coping with our problems or situations and it takes the edge off.

In our case, it helped the trip seem that much more enjoyable and so much shorter.

Now I offer you, The Deer Hunter.

Hau!
(for Dave West and Dave Bald Eagle)

THE DEER HUNTER

A Short Story
by
Eya Mani

The men had been standing around telling stories, funny stories, sometimes silly stories about the old times and how some of the old ones dealt with problems.

And sometimes logic and common sense isn't always the best policy.

Anyway, they say the old one had been living alone outside the village for as long as anyone could remember.

Living alone.

Never bothering anyone.

Never speaking to anyone.

Never going to town.

But forever busy.

Doing things important only to him.

One day the village had a new pastor to replace the one that was retiring. It was said the new pastor knew how to speak the language, and speak it fluently too!

This meant trouble for the old one.

He just knew that the new pastor would be visiting him any day now, and he was right!

The preacher came in the evening and didn't stay long.

He met the old one outside his log house and greeted him and introduced himself.

Then he asked the old one to come the next Sunday for church. There would be a village picnic and he would get a chance to meet everyone then.

The old one reluctantly agreed to be there, and so the preacher left feeling good about himself.

When Sunday came, the old one stood outside his house and waited until he saw the last person go into the church before he left his house.

He intended to find a seat in the back.

Way in the back where he wouldn't be noticed.

He had never attended a white mans church before, so he knew it would be different!

When he entered, he was surprised to see everyone seated in the back.

The entire back of the church was filled and the only seating he could find was way up in front.

Up in front.

This was not good.

As he took his seat he knew everyone was watching him, he could feel their eyes on him and it made the hair on his neck stand up.

After he had taken his seat, the pastor greeted him loudly, bringing more attention to him.

He didn't like that.

Then, just as church services were about to start, two young ladies came in and seated themselves directly in front of the old one.

The pastor asked everyone to rise for opening prayer, and they did so.

Not knowing why everyone had stood up, the old one also stood up and looked around.

Everyone had their head down and their eyes were closed so he too put his head down, but he kept one eye open to see what the others were going to do.

After prayer everyone was seated again, and the old one found himself wondering what it was he had come for.

The pastor was wearing a white robe and he was speaking in a language he had never heard before, but he knew it was not the white man's language!

The people were asked again to rise and again everyone had their heads down and their eyes closed.

The old one was not used to this.

When he prayed to the Creator, he prayed with his head uplifted and his arms outstretched asking for guidance and strength.

He was not used to this so he let his mind, then his eyes wander.

He didn't know what he could let his eyes rest on but he found the young woman in front of him to be very good to look upon.

He remembered his youth and such a woman!

The people were seated again.

And they stood again.

And again the old one let his eyes wander, and he soon found himself noticing certain things about her!

His eyes took in the smallness of her waist and the roundness of her hips.

Then his eyes came to rest on her buttocks.

But this was troubling!

Her dress was stuffed between her buttocks!

She must be in real discomfort!

Long ago, he too had known such discomfort.

The old one turned slowly around to see if anyone was watching, but all were in the ashamed posture yet!

Good!

He had to help her!

No wait!

He had to think about this!!

What if he did help her and someone saw?

They might think badly of him.

How would he live then?

What would they say?

Wait, he had to think, once when he was young he had such an experience!

He had been hunting the very elusive white-tailed deer.

He had run a great distance and now he was getting close to his quarry.

Moving slowly through the buck brush, hunched over with his bow and arrow at the ready, moving ever so slowly.

Then he realized it!

It had been bothering him for sometime now.

He had a Bite!

The leather breech cloth he wore had worked its way up between his buttocks and he was getting very sore, and the feeling was a burning sensation because of the sweat.

Yes!

She must be feeling that way by now!

Very great discomfort!

And she, a woman!

He had to help!

The people could say nothing if they knew that he was helping a woman, could they?

The people were seated again for a time before they were asked to rise again.

This gave the old one time to ponder this most delicate and important matter.

He was a Lakota warrior!

Protector of women and children!

A Keeper of the Law!

At all costs! He must protect the women and children from harm!

The people had to understand!

He must do this thing!

The people all rose again and hung their heads and closed their eyes.

With best intentions, the old one reached down and pulled out the dress material.

In a flash the young woman whirled and slapped him across the face.

Whack!

The old one turned quickly to see if anyone had seen what had just happened.

Good!

No one moved an eyelid!

He was safe.

He had relieved her discomfort but she had reacted in a most peculiar way!

Young people!

HUH!

He was indignant!

Such thanklessness!

As he stood thinking about this he thought better of it.

Maybe he should have left well enough alone?

Maybe he should have left her to her discomfort?

After all, she was a woman.

Who can tell what a woman might think?

Without thinking about it the old one reached down and pushed the dress material back in, giving her back her bite!!!

Hau!
(for Dave West and Dave Bald Eagle)

WATEHICA

From the Author

As I write this next offering, another of our respected elders has gone on to make the journey alone, and this brings to mind the rest of our relatives and friends who have also left us and gone on alone.

What have they left us?

What tracks have they left so we and the others may follow?

This also brings another questions forward.

What am I leaving for my children? Will they be able to see my footprints? Have they listened while I tried to teach them what I was taught?

Probably the most troubling question I have is what kind of life will they have after I also take my leave of them and go on alone?

My grandfather was a veteran of the United States Army and the United States Air Force during the Second World War and Korea.

After his discharge, he was promised a 'bonus' from the United States Government for his outstanding service to his country in two wars.

In our next story, we find him waiting and waiting and waiting. Finally to make ends meet, he finally has to sell off his most prized possessions, his team of Belgian horses.

We will get just a glimpse into the final hours of that event and of what my uncle shared with me. Leaving forever indelible in my mind the sort of men they were and of what was most important to them, with their humility and quiet strength.

I hope I could have such character.

But now, my next offering...

WATEHICA (That Which You Hold Dear)

Hau!
(for my Uncle Elmer and Grandpa Charlie)

WATEHICA

(That which you hold dear)

A Short Story
by
Eya Mani

It was still dark out, and the little boy had been quietly sitting on his grandfather's lap. He had his head on his grandfather's chest and he could hear his heartbeat and he could hear him breathing.

Occasionally his grandfather would take a deep breath and sigh.

Despite the boys age of 4 years, he knew his favorite grandfather was troubled about something he didn't want to do, and this translated to the boy and he too felt bad.

Everyone in the log house was still asleep, but his grandfather was an early riser and he had gotten up early as usual, lit one of the kerosene lamps that stood on the table in the middle of the room.

Then he lit a fire in grandma's favorite wood stove and here they sat, the two of them, feeling bad about some thing.

The boy sat watching the reflection of the dancing flames on the wall, from the open door on the wood stove and he thought about his grandfather.

When he and his grandfather went after a load of wood, his grandfather would gather only those smaller dry branches of cottonwood and tell the young boy, "This is the best wood for making bread, grandma sure likes to use this kind of wood when she cooks and makes fresh bread."

So they had two piles of wood, one pile had larger branches his grandfather would saw into blocks for heating, and the other, the kind grandma liked to cook with.

The boy turned to his grandfather and straightened his shirt collar, then he hugged him and got off his lap and went outside.

The village was still dark but the dawn was breaking and he could barely make out the smoke slowly rising from the other log houses in the village.

The birds had been up raising a ruckus for a while now in the trees down below the place. Then the dogs started to bark and wake up the rest of the village.

This was the best part of the day.

Smoke smells from the houses, the birds started singing, dogs were barking, and the smell of coffee brewing and food cooking filled the air.

There was activity in the corrals down below the house, and someone was whistling a tune, so he strained his eyes to see what was going on down there.

It was his uncle Elmer.

He had already hitched up his grandfather's team of Belgian horses to the wagon, and now he was loading an empty 50 gallon drum onto the wagon, along with a pitchfork and a manure fork and an empty water bucket.

Then while the boy watched, he drove the wagon up to the house and got down, and they both went inside.

This was his favorite uncle too, and he was never quiet!

He slammed the heavy door as he came inside and as he walked, he stepped heavily on the wooden floor, making sure he woke those who were still sleeping.

He greeted the old ones.

Then he asked if the coffee was ready and if there was anything ready to eat.

Without anyone answering he poured himself a cup of coffee and made a sandwich of roast deer meat.

Everyone spoke the language and the boy listened intently, not wanting to miss anything discussed.

Maybe he would find out why his grandfather's heart was so heavy.

When there was a break in the discussion, he asked his uncle what he was going to do today with the pitchforks and the barrel in the wagon.

"Fish Friday" his uncle said loudly, then laughing even louder he continued, "Who ever heard?"

Then he said, "When the meat runs out, then we have fish, there's always something for us if we get up early and go after it."

"If you want to catch fish in a hurry, get ready, I'll show you how to catch the biggest ones without a line and hook, and without getting wet either, and we won't be long."

"Shall I wake the others then?"

"No, let them sleep. Maybe they need their rest. Maybe someday they'll be able to buy their fish instead of catching it, but come, let's go before the sun comes up."

As they bounced along the wagon road leading to the river he still felt bad because his grandfather was quiet that morning.

They had read the Bible with grandma and had said prayers but that still didn't seem to make him feel any better.

Usually grandpa felt better after his prayers were said, but not this morning.

As they neared the river crossing, his uncle turned the team into the deepest part of the river and drove the wagon into the water, then he stopped the horses when the water was up to the bottom of the wagon box.

All the while his uncle was whistling and humming and the boy liked that.

He remembered some of the tunes from the old radio his grandmother had.

She had grandpa hookup the old dry cell battery and stretch out the wire antennae for reception. Then they would listen to the "World Today" and "Paul Harvey".

Then grandpa would take the radio apart again and put it away.

Sometimes they would listen to KOLY 1300 AM in Mobridge, but only when one of his uncles was playing guitar and singing gospel hymns on Sundays. When they sang songs, even the neighbors came to listen and sometimes everyone would sing along.

His uncle rolled a smoke and sat quietly until he finished his smoke.

The boy knew enough not to talk when they were fishing, or to move around either, but his uncle didn't seem to follow the rules and the boy wondered how were they ever going to catch any fish if his uncle wasn't quiet?

His uncle picked up the pitchfork and shouted, "Here they come!"

The boy hadn't noticed before but the fishes where already swimming around the wagon and team.

His uncle had been waiting for the really big catfish to swim by, and now they were coming and he was ready.

With their heads swinging from side to side, as if on parade they seemed to be showing off, the huge catfish came, seeming to offer themselves to the man with the pitchfork.

The boy had to take a deep breath, he had never seen catfish this big before, and there were so many!

When he was lucky to be asked to go fishing with his older brothers, he had only caught the "pan-size" on his homemade fishing pole.

""This one is for Mrs. Grey Eagle, this one is for Old Frank, this one is for Mrs. Bears Rib, and this one is for my sister."

He went on naming people who were going to have fish that day, and one after another the fish came and he speared them with the pitchfork and tossed them into the barrel.

After the sun topped the east hill the fish all went under water at once, as if on command.

When the fish stopped coming, his uncle took the water bucket from under the seat and filled the barrel with river water, then he rolled another smoke and sat quietly watching the smoke rise in the calm cool air.

"And that's how you catch the really big ones." His uncle shouted as he turned the team around in the water, and he laughed his belly laugh and he started whistling again.

"But you have to get up early enough to get ready, and just make sure you get enough for everyone. No one goes hungry when you can feed everyone." His uncle had said as the horses started to trot.

They always knew when they were going home the boy thought.

The boy was standing, holding onto the barrel watching the catfish move around, and he ventured a question.

"Uncle, why is grandpa thinking so hard?"

His uncle hesitated, measuring his reply.

"Sometimes we have to do things we don't want to do. Grandpa has to make a decision today, but he knows best. I wanted to show you this before it was too late, now what ever will happen will happen."

The boy and his uncle made the rounds delivering the early morning prize.

When they came back to the house just before the noon meal, he knew.

There was a big truck waiting at the corral.

Now he knew why grandpa was so sad.

Hau!
(for uncle Elmer and grandpa Charlie)

LOST VALLEY

(from the Author)

As a young man I had hunted in Lost Valley many times. The mule deer we found there seemed to offer themselves to us and they always appeared to be well fed and they were plentiful.

Although I didn't know the significance of this place back then, I did know that we only went there to hunt as a last resort. When game couldn't be found elsewhere, after much deliberation and preparation, my grandfather would take us there.

Things have changed.

As my People have become less dependent on the Creator and more dependent on their own abilities to provide for their families by other means, these stories and legends have become just that, however mostly forgotten.

Before my grandfather left, we took one last trip back to Lost Valley.

Without speaking, we found everything just as the old man had said in his story of the 40 hunted.

As we stood and looked down from where the alter was made, I could imagine the People camped down below, and I could feel the reverence and the peace of that place.

On leaving that place, all my grandfather would say about that brave young man who gave his life for his People was, "they buried him and his horse so no one would find the bodies."

As I share this tale of love and sacrifice with you, I think that perhaps someone, someday, may have need of the Lost Valley again, and the Creator's ability to provide whatever that someone may need, whatever it may be.

And now, I offer you, LOST VALLEY.

HAU!

LOST VALLEY

A Short story
by
Eya Mani

I had come to visit the old one before, many times. On these short visits, I usually brought him fresh meat and salt and sugar. Sometimes he'd ask for shells for his rifle, and a few times I brought him a bottle of soda or hard candy.

Most people called him Earth Eater, but I think it was a bad translation of the Lakota word Hoka (Badger).

And the way some of them said his name, Earth Eater.

It was with disdain.

You could almost feel the animosity.

I think that was because most of them had to rent land from him, but I also think this was because not many people took the time to understand him.

While he was alive, I didn't have any opinion about the way he wore his clothes either.

But now, when I think about him, I think he didn't like wearing the white man's clothes.

Nothing seemed to fit him very well.

I always had the impression that when I left him, he would throw off his white man's clothes and put on his Lakota clothing.

I could be wrong, but it was a thought or a feeling I had about him.

This old man lived out beyond Black Horse and Lodge Pole, along a small creek emptying into the Grand River.

I would leave our house before dawn, usually empty handed, but when I arrived at his place I would have freshly killed game for him. He loved fresh prairie chickens and pheasant.

He usually told me if he wanted anything when I came for my next visit, and I always did my best to bring what he wanted.

Sometimes my grandfather would throw in the hard candy or the bottle of soda.

Although he never said so, I know this old man appreciated it.

I found that when I brought him these small gifts, he would often share a tale of long ago with me.

Although he always had almost no work for me to do for him, he sometimes wanted visitors.

And although he never said so either, it was just a feeling I got from him, so he and I worked out a system.

On my visits, if he didn't start telling me a story within the first 15 or 20 minutes of my arrival, I did what I could for him, then I'd leave.

If he wanted me to stay, he would usually tell me a story about long ago.

On this day, he had hot coffee waiting for me.

I never did figure out how he knew when I was coming either, because I only came when I could get away. And how did grandpa know when I was going out to check on the old man?

As I rode into his place, I saw him sitting on a wood block in front of a campfire. He was putting another piece of wood on the coals.

As I dismounted, he picked up the coffee pot and poured two cups of really strong black coffee.

After I unsaddled my horse and let him graze on a short rope, I sat on the wood block he offered, and I took the coffee he handed me.

Then he began the story.

It bothered me that he seemed to be in a hurry to tell me this story, because he didn't bother to greet me.

We usually went through the ritual of formal greetings, then he would ask me about all the news since my last visit.

But this time it was very different, he just started right in.

"One day I had gotten up extra early. I don't know why but I just didn't feel right, something inside of me just didn't feel right."

"I knew something was definitely amiss."

I took a sip of the strong black coffee and it drew an involuntary face from me, which he saw while he was speaking, but he paid no attention. He kept right on talking, so I set the cup down and gave him my full attention as the story continued.

"On my way up the hill to get the horses we had staked out, I noticed that there was a lot of grasshoppers. Lots and lots of grasshoppers. There were so many grasshoppers, the horses had stopped eating and they were milling around stomping their feet. I guess they were trying to keep the grasshoppers from climbing up their legs and from eating their manes and their tails."

"I know I had to brush them off the tether rope that tied off each of the horses. I was sure they were eating it."

"All the way to the river I could hear them crunch under my feet as we walked along."

"Grasshoppers usually get out of your way as you approach, but these just stayed put. So I and the horses just crunched our way down to the river, and as the horses drank their fill from the mud puddle that our river had become, and as the morning got brighter, I had a chance to take a better look around."

"Where sweet clover had grown before in abundance, along the river banks and up the draws and small ravines along the hillsides, there was now only dry, dying stems."

"The sweet clover, the young cotton woods, the willow groves, the plum and choke cherry bushes. Everything was being eaten, even the buck brush and the sage, nothing was spared."

"Everything seemed to be alive as these grasshoppers moved around, eating their way down through the outer tree bark of the branches and leaving the trees and wild fruit bushes bare."

"Once these trees and bushes were exposed, they would all eventually die."

"My grandparents had told us stories about these things before. They said that this happens every once in awhile. They said it had to happen, to keep things in balance. The new would replace the old, and not all of this was bad, because we would be provided for if we really needed help."

"About the only thing I could think of that was good about this, was there would be more fire wood for me to cut after these grasshoppers left, because my grandfather also had said, 'a lean winter would be sure to follow'."

"I didn't have to say anything about this when I came home from the river because everyone was already up and about, talking about it this morning."

"One of my uncles was sitting outside under the Shade with a couple of boxes of rounds, he was shooting the grasshoppers off the out house and the garden fence posts with a rifle."

"That's how big some of them were, you could see them at over a hundred feet away."

"My grandmother fixed breakfast, and as the rest of us ate in silence, she told us a story of times like this. The things the People did when the grasshoppers, and sometimes the crickets came and didn't leave after staying a week or longer."

"Grandpa said they rarely last over a day or two, but sometimes they come and would never leave until they themselves will eventually starve to death."

"He said in his lifetime, this is only the second time he'd seen them, and he was surprised about that too. I guess these kinds of things were more prevalent down in the southwest where they already have deserts, but up here where we have snow and very cold winters, this thing is almost unheard of."

"I was surprised at the speed with which they'd arrived too."

"We had not heard anything during the night to indicate they'd come. Anyway, I was grateful I guess, that I was able to see this happen, or that I was allowed to experience this, because of what would happen later."

"Grandma said that when this happens, extreme heat and a drought usually follow for the rest of the summer and fall, and if no snow should come that winter, everyone will be in trouble come next spring."

"And so it was that the grasshoppers all died, and the smell of them was very bad."

"It was sickening."

"The death smell is a sweet dead smell that you will always remember. It makes your stomach turn."

"So we had a very hard winter, and when spring came, there was no three day drizzles like when I was a small boy. Only the hot sun and the hot winds and the never ending dust. This was followed by the never ending hunger and thirst that comes with drought."

"We knew we were in bad shape, because there was no game around."

"Then one day my grandfather came back from sitting on the hill."

"He said, 'There is help for us, because the Creator will provide for us. We only have to prepare for this gift. Those who will be going with me, you must tell no one. If others are worthy, they will ask the Creator and he will provide for them as he will provide for us'."

"So with that, he prepared a sweat lodge for purifying those who would take this journey with him. He also joked that we had no need to fast, since we had been fasting for some time now."

"But we must also purify our horses and our wagons, our weapons and everything we are taking with us, everything."

"And so we did."

"We purified everything we had to take on the journey."

"As we headed west at dawn the next day, grandpa told us to only think good thoughts, and to pray and give thanks for this great gift that we were about to receive, and so we did."

"I think I prayed every step of the way out there."

"It was an hour into the ride on the third day that my grandfather stopped on a hill overlooking the river which lay to the north."

"To the west as far as we could see were lush ravines and draws full of many kinds of grasses and wild fruits. The trees were full of leaves and wild flowers were growing so thick, you could smell them from way up yonder where we had stopped to wonder at all this."

"One of my uncles could not believe his eyes or his ears, because he almost shouted out loud, 'How can this be? We know that there is a drought, look behind from where we have come. Everything is dead'."

"We camped up on the hill that night, and it was miserable."

"We wanted to get down there and start filling the wagons with wild fruit, and my uncles wanted to start bringing down these huge mule deer we had seen earlier that morning when we had first arrived. Those mule deer that my grandmother loved so much, but my grandfather would not. He held us fast with these words."

"'Everything is now changed.'"

"'One of you has changed it all. Everything! Because you would not believe what you have been told, and what you have seen, everything is now changed.'"

"And with that, he left us standing on the hill."

"He himself went down the hill and disappeared out of sight into the river bottom, and he did not return until almost dark."

"When he came back he told us that he was to go and sit on the hill for three more days, if he had the strength. And we only had until his strength was gone, to gather, and to hunt and to dry our meat, and to dig the wild turnips that were so plentiful just a hundred yards down the hill leading into the valley."

"So at dawn the next day, he went to the south and skirted the draws and then he went west again, until he found a place on the highest hill. He made sure it was a place where we could see him easily no matter where we were down below. And as he was making his alter on top, we were already digging feverishly at the turnips since they were right here."

"When we had thought we had enough turnips, two of us then went and started to fill the wagons with wild fruit of every kind."

"The plums and cherries were so big and juicy, and sweet, you would not believe how sweet those plums and cherries were."

The old man paused here and took a sip of his coffee, and he also made a face. He set his cup down, ran his shirt sleeve across his mouth and he continued.

"But we made sure we had lots of every kind of fruit, especially the wild grapes that my grandmother loved so much, and that are so hard to find."

"By sundown of the first day, we had one wagon filled with the very best fruit and turnips that we could find, and my grandpa was still standing on his feet with his arms stretched towards the heavens."

"We also prayed as we worked, until it got too dark for us to see him."

"It was then that the uncle who had doubted said, 'We will eat no food that we have taken from this place until we are done, because our father is suffering, we too will suffer with him'."

"And so it was that we all went to sleep with more hunger than I've ever known."

"We were so tired that we all fell asleep very soon. And in the morning when we awoke, we found that we were ourselves somehow refreshed."

"When my grandfather stood back up to pray the next morning, my uncles then started the hunt. They brought in those big beautiful mule deer that my grandmother loves so much. And I prayed as I made pa'pa' (dried meat)."

"I was cutting the meat so thin that you could almost see through it. But this was to make sure that none of it would spoil before we got it home."

"It was during the dressing of the second mule deer buck that they appeared. The dark clouds first appeared on the horizon behind my grandfather, down towards the south."

"And then I noticed that my grandfather had fallen down. We could see him trying to stand up. When he finally did rise again to his feet and stretch out his arms again, the clouds went away."

"And we worked and prayed even harder then before."

"Toward the late afternoon of the second day, my grandfather had fallen down again. And this time he could not get back up, so the dark clouds were coming again, with much lightening and the thunder was booming."

"We were getting very afraid, because those clouds looked like they were boiling in toward us."

"Then we saw him rise up again, and it seemed with renewed strength, because those clouds just went away like someone had blown them clear out of the sky, and we were very glad, and we worked even that much harder."

"My grandfather stood until the sun went down, and as we finished our work, we thought we might have enough meat and other foods now."

"We were afraid that my grandfather would die up on that hill, trying to save us from starvation and my uncles had to discuss this at some length."

"Two of them thought they should go and bring him down now, but it was the oldest, the uncle who had doubted, he stopped them."

"He said, 'We have been given a blessing, I know that the Creator has forgiven me my foolishness. Let us not add to that foolishness by thinking we know more than our father. He will come when he knows we have enough. There is only one more day left, let us finish this the way he would want us to finish it'."

"So they agreed, and we again went to sleep with even greater hunger than we had the night before."

"But again, in the morning, we were refreshed as we were on the other morning we were there."

"It was on the third day. We had just finished dressing out our third mule deer buck, when my grandfather came into the camp we had made."

"He told one of my uncles to go down and bring in that mule deer buck that was taking its water down by the river."

"And so he went and brought it back. After he returned, they dressed it and we had a feast that evening."

"We ate fresh picked wild fruit of every kind, we had fresh Tapi (liver) and talo (the choicest meats)."

"We even made wahumpi (soup) with some of the new turnips and mule deer ribs."

"It was the best meal I had in a very long time, but we ate slowly and we all had our fill."

"After supper, I asked my grandfather how he knew about this place, but he said he was tired now. He would tell it to me on the way home. Now all he wanted to do was to rest."

"The next morning when I awoke, there was a roast above the fire and my grandfather had just finished making the sweat lodge."

"We were to purify ourselves again before we left the valley. And so we did as we had done before we had begun our journey into this valley."

"After we purified the wagons, and the horses, and everything we had brought with us, we went down into the river to take a swim in the cool clear refreshing waters."

"As we ate our last meal in the valley that morning, a sudden gust of wind came up and my grandfather stopped eating."

"He sat and listened as if someone was talking to him. Then he said, 'it happened right here.'"

"'There was forty of them, mostly old ones, and women and children. And there was only thirteen warriors to protect them.'"

"'There was some men on horses, the long knives, who were after them, and so they came into this valley, and they stopped right here.'"

"'Their leader was a young man, great in strength and great in courage and in wisdom. Only through his skill did he keep his struggling party ahead of the long knives.'"

"'But their horses were getting weak from lack of food and the old ones were suffering. A few of the children and a few of the old ones were very sick and it was the old ones who begged to be left behind so the others could escape, but their leader would not.'"

"'Their leader told them to set up camp right here, in this very spot. Then he and a few of his warriors went to scout and to get some meat for their People.'"

"'If we die, we will die together. But we will not die hungry,' he told his People. Then he went up there where I made my alter, and he made his alter."

"'He sat up there all night, he and his horse.'"

"'That night the long knives came riding through the camp.'"

"'They rode right by the tethered horses and they rode right by the makeshift shelters, and the People sat and watched them ride by.'"

"'They were very afraid. But it was as if they could not be seen by these soldiers, the long knives. And it seemed that although the long knives' horses could see them, the long knives could not.'"

"'The long knives rode right through their camp and pitched their own camp just below there, where we took our swim. And in the morning they continued their search for these, our People, but they had lost their tracks.'"

"'It was as if they had just disappeared into the air.'"

"'When the young men went to tell their leader the good news, they found that he and his horse were dead.'"

"'They were drained of all their blood. All around them the ground appeared to be red, but it was completely covered with mosquitoes which had engorged themselves with the blood of this young man and his horse.'"

"'When we leave here, you will not find this place again, because it is a place set aside for those who want help. It is a place set aside for those who are willing to sacrifice themselves for that help, but that help must be meant for others, as that young man had intended.'"

"'Now, we must cover this food and we must not let sunlight touch any of it until we get it home. Then we must let grandma do with it what she does.'"

"And so we covered the food and we came home. No one spoke on the way home either. I think we were all so thankful that in our silence we were all praying and giving thanks."

The story was finished.

Earth Eater stood up abruptly, signifying that the story was ended.

He picked up his pot of strong black coffee and put out the campfire with the contents.

I too stood up and dumped out my cup, having not drunk a second time because it was much too strong for me.

I asked him about it, if that story was truly real...

But he only smiled at me and he went back into his house and closed the door.

I saddled up old Smokey and I rode home slowly, thinking about what he had just told me.

"Wow" I thought. "It was just like watching a movie."

When I got home, grandpa came to the barn while I was unsaddling Old Smokey and he asked me, "So what did the old man have to say?"

"Did he mention Lost Valley?"

I could hear him chuckling as he left me and Old Smokey looking after him.

Hau!

IYO'HI

(The Journey)

A DIVISION OF ARTICLES

(from the Author)

In putting together my next offering, I had to do some soul searching because it contains some material that some people might not deem printable, merely because of what it speaks.

Going back and recreating YAMNI, I felt in my heart that there would be no danger of speaking on this subject, because it's a generalization of what was actually said and of what actually took place. Yet in my alteration and narration of events, I believe that I have managed to leave the main thoughts and the ideas intact to keep the story interesting and entertaining.

In WANJI the loss of a friend in a most unexpected and unusual way causes me to pause and ask why our society has remained unchanged in almost 50 years.

In the beginning of this new century, in another border town a young man with a visible handicap was fed alcohol, and when he passed out he was placed in a garbage can upside down.

He regurgitated the alcohol and breathed it back into his lungs. Consequently he died and again no one was charged with a crime because the four young people responsible for his death were also from prominent members of the community, and they also claimed that they were "just having fun".

And now my next offering, A DIVISION OF ARTICLES.

IYO'HI

(The Journey)
by
Eya Mani
A Division of Articles

WANJI

It was the summer I will never forget. I would turn 16 that July and I thought life was passing me by. Like many young people I wanted to learn more, about my People, about the old ways, and mostly about our way of life.

I soon found out that I couldn't learn anything from the kids my age, so I turned to the older male relatives in my family.

They had already taught me how to rope and ride, and how to break and cut horses alone. And to make sure I had a good work ethic, they also taught me how to operate and maintain farm and ranching machinery.

They told me, with my knowledge, my experience, and my ability, I would eventually be able to go anywhere and get a good steady job.

I already knew that a good reputation was a powerful thing.

A few of my grandfathers, with the help of their sons, had built reputations as breeders of quality cattle.

They fed only natural feeds and native grasses and they refused using any additives or hormones to stimulate their growth as many other cattle producers were doing. But most importantly, we made sure that the cattle always had plenty of good fresh drinking water.

The care and attention we gave our cattle paid off.

When the Standing Rock calf sales were mentioned on the radio in the fall, many cattle buyers would show up and without seeing my grandparent's herds, they would buy their entire calf crop at very good prices.

Many of them would return year after year to buy their calves.

I wouldn't know it then, but like most stories, anything bad or unusual that's going to happen, usually starts out looking pretty normal.

I am the youngest of three brothers.

My brothers had already made themselves known as good dependable workers. So when spring came and it was time for planting, a few of the more prosperous farmers would come and seek them out to put in their crops and do summer fallow.

That summer their boss needed an extra hand, so after I had finished my work at home, I went up to stay at my mom's place in Lemmon, while I went to work with my brothers.

My brothers would ride those big farm tractors in the day time, and I would ride one during the night.

The crops had to be planted as quickly as possible, so we made it a 24 hour operation.

We would stop long enough to refill the drill, check the fluids in the tractor, tighten any loose bolts and grease the equipment.

My brothers made sure that I got the message, "time was money", so we spent as little time as possible with something they called down time.

We even ate our lunch while making our rounds.

We all stayed in a bunkhouse behind mom's house, on the outskirts of one of the border towns a few miles away from our reservation.

One morning after my shift was finished, the boss picked me up at work and commented that he didn't think anyone would be working that day. He dropped me off at the driveway leading up the hill to mom's place.

The vibrations of the tractor had made my body feel numb, so as I walked along I was trying to work the circulation back into my legs, arms and hands.

I was tired and dirty and I needed some sleep, but I wouldn't be getting any rest that day.

As I approached the house, I saw one of my brothers sitting beneath a tree outside the bunk house.

He was smoking a cigarette and drinking a beer.

This was unusual.

My brothers were supposed to be at work.

"Hey, what's wrong? Aren't you supposed to be some place this morning? Did someone call the day off or what?"

"Awww bullshit!" he fired back throwing his empty beer can into the burn barrel.

I knew this brother was angry and probably drunk, and not wishing to have a confrontation, I went into the bunk house and took a shower.

Then I changed into clean clothes.

Breakfast was usually ready by now, so I entered the main house through the back door into the kitchen.

All I could smell was coffee brewing.

"Guess there'll be no breakfast today either." I thought as I made my way into the living room.

My mother was sitting on the living room sofa with one of her closest friends.

They were holding each other and they were softly crying into each others shoulders. When she saw me she shouted, "THEY KILLED HIM SONNY!"

"Those sons-a-bitches killed him."

Her words trailed off into more tears of anguish, and they both broke out into sounds of renewed agony.

Without saying a word, and not knowing what had caused this outburst, I went back into the kitchen and poured a cup of steaming black coffee.

Then I walked outside to the front porch where my step father was sitting smoking a cigarette.

As I sat down I said,

"Good morning dad, what's mom talking about? Who did they kill?"

My step father slowly put out his cigarette and I moved a lawn chair a little closer, so I could sit beside him.

"Good morning Sonny."

He sat quietly looking into the distance, then he slowly took out another cigarette from the pack in his shirt pocket, then he lit it and took a deep breath.

After he expelled the smoke he said softly,

"Bobby."

"They killed Bobby last night."

It was my turn to make an outburst!

"Holy shit!"

I couldn't contain my surprise.

"Who killed him?"

"What happened?"

After another long pause, he spoke very softly,

"Some kids from town got a holt of Bobby and painted him."

I could feel the pain and anger in his words as I sat back in my chair trying to get my thoughts in order.

I was still tired from the previous nights work.

After my step father finished putting out his half smoked cigarette, he continued in short sentences.

"Just like in that movie."

"And he died."

"He suffocated..and he died."

My mind was reeling.

"Painted him?"

I had to think a minute.

I was tired and sleepy, but now, hearing what had happened to one of my friends, I came fully wide awake.

Then I remembered that movie.

It was GOLD FINGER, with James Bond.

In that movie the bad guy gets James Bond's girlfriend and paints her gold.

By the time James Bond finds her, she is already dead, because she suffocates.

Her body can't breathe through her painted skin, so she dies.

And all this time I had thought it was just made up stuff for the movie.

I slowly finished my coffee and set the cup down.

I had to think about this, and as I thought more of Bobby, a sadness slowly came over me.

Bobby had been a childhood friend of mine.

His mother had married a rancher and they lived just south of here down by Meadow.

Bobby and I had grown up together back on the reservation.

Back home, you could always tell when Bobby was around.

His strong nasal voice with a country twang could be heard echoing up and down the valley every morning and most of the day when he was out doors.

It didn't matter what he was doing.

He could be hauling water, chopping wood or returning from the river with the days catch.

He was always singing at the top of his lungs.

Bobby had been a gentle person and I had taken him as a friend, mostly for his own protection than for anything else, at first.

Kids can be cruel, and without someone's help I'm sure Bobby would have been living in a small hell.

Some of the other kids would make fun of his singing and they would make him cry. And if any of his sisters came to try and help him, they would also be made fun of and sometimes they would be beaten.

As I sat thinking about him, I had an over powering feeling of guilt too.

Before I became one of Bobbie's few friends, I too had made fun of his singing, but that's where it stopped.

Sometimes the kids would chase him home after school, but in this I had never taken part. And as I thought about this a little more, I came to the conclusion that this was one of the reasons I chose not to be around kids my own age.

After we had become friends, some of the other kids gradually accepted him as he was, to the point that on a few occasions, some of the other boys would join in and we'd do his back up vocals.

The song Duke of Earl was our favorite.

Once after we'd finished singing with him one of the other boys said,

"You know Bobby? We ought to start a group."

Bobby thought this was hysterical, he couldn't get over it.

And I could see the change in him too. He was pleased with who he was even if the road had been bumpy at first.

Then his mother had married and they had moved and I very seldom ever saw him again. But when I did I could still see that new brightness in his eyes, and I always felt good about that.

Now as I sat and thought about it, I felt a new sadness about that.

I wondered just how far Bobby would have gone if he'd had a chance. A real chance.

Now Bobby was gone.

"Do they know who done it?"

My step father pulled out a pint of Old Crow and took a long pull on it and recapped it.

Then after he set it down between his feet he lit another cigarette.

He breathed the smoke in deeply and as he expelled the smoke, he said "Yeah."

"It was the cops' kid, the mayors' kid, and a few other big wigs' kids in town."

"They said they was only having fun."

"They said they didn't know that he would die."

After sitting awhile in angered silence, I picked up my cup.

"Well, that's it."

"I wanna go home now."

"Can you take me out past the airport? I'll walk home from there."

Following me back into the house he said,

"I can take you home, sure you don't want a ride all the way?"

"No thanks dad, mom will need you here. Can you tell the boss to mail my check to me? We just about got it done anyway. The other guys can finish up for him if they want."

"I just wanna go home now."

After my step father had left me off about eight miles out of town, I started for home, walking in the ditch, some times I would wave rides by.

I needed to be alone now and walking made me feel better.

I didn't want a ride just yet, even though there was still about 42 miles or so to go before I got home.

"Home."

"What a funny word."

"Almost everyone I knew called my grandparents' place "home."

NUMPA

The pickup truck was coming from behind. I thought I could tell whose truck it was when it first came within hearing range.

I guessed it was two, maybe three miles behind me yet.

When it topped the hills, the sounds the tires made on the blacktop got louder, and when it went down into the low spots I wasn't able to hear it any longer.

But from those sounds I could estimate its distance and speed.

After a minute or so, I moved farther off the road.

When the pickup truck topped the last rise, I could hear the truck gear down, and I knew it was going to stop.

"I know that truck" I thought.

"Geez! Even out in the middle of nowhere a guy can't be alone!"

When the truck slowed down enough, the driver matched my speed, then someone shouted out the open window.

"There you are, I stopped by your mom's place, but she said you'd just left."

"Wanna lift?"

"I know that voice."

Without looking up I knew who it was.

It was that sickeningly beautiful young woman.

The one whose husband had gotten hurt a few years ago.

"No thank you. I just wanna go home now. Thank you anyway."

"Aw come on now," she said as she dropped another gear.

"My husband told me to find you. It'll just be for a few days, I promise."

"You'll be finished in a few days, then we'll take you home. I promise."

As I walked along I thought about them. I had worked for them before, more than a few times.

Her husband was paralyzed from the waist down and he was now confined to a wheel chair.

Someone had once told me it had been a farm accident, but my elders had often said that there was no such things as accidents.

When I thought of this I could feel a spark of anger in the pit of my stomach.

I didn't know why I could feel this way about that crippled young man.

Maybe there was such a thing as accidents.

"It must be because of what happened to Bobby," I thought as I walked along.

These were a younger farm couple, probably in their mid twenties or early thirties, and they had no children.

They usually came after me or one of my brothers when they needed help.

But lately, it seemed they came after me more often than not, especially lately.

I didn't have to think about it long.

I remember grandma once telling me that work answers all prayers.

Besides, these two had always been good to me.

After I put my bag in the back with her groceries, I climbed into the cab and she drove on to their place.

We didn't talk much after I got in.

But I knew she was taking quick little peeks and longer glances at me while she drove on.

She probably didn't think I'd notice.

But I did.

After driving for an hour or so, we arrived at the woman's farm.

First, I helped carry in the groceries, then on my way out she called after me, "dinner will be ready in two hours, okay?"

I went to put my bag in the bunkhouse.

I liked working here.

The bunkhouse always had a woman's touch.

Matching curtains hung from the clean windows and the beds always had fresh sheets, blankets and pillow cases on them.

And after work when I took my shower, I always knew there would be a stack of fresh towels piled high in the closet behind the door.

I usually felt at ease around my boss' and their wives, because chances were, I had already worked for them before and I already knew what had to be done.

But this time I felt uneasy about being here, I like something was out of place, like I was being brought here for another reason other than work.

And I knew they both felt my uneasiness as well.

I could feel it the moment I climbed into the cab with her, something was different this time.

I felt her eyes looking me over when she thought I wouldn't notice, but I had caught her staring and she blushed with embarrassment, and it made her grind the gears crossing the creek just below their place.

Then I wondered if she had noticed me stealing glances at her?

I felt embarrassed about it.

What if she had noticed?

She did know.

Just as I knew.

What if she told her husband?

When I thought of her husband, I could feel that anger move around in the pit of my stomach again.

"Maybe I shouldn't have come here," I thought as I left the bunkhouse to start work.

To keep my mind off the woman, I thought of Bobby.

When that didn't work, I tried to think of grandma and remember some of the things that she'd taught me.

But I was growing confused, so I said another prayer for Bobby instead.

During the noon meal my despair turned into more than clumsiness.

It could have been the way she was dressed.

She had changed into tight fitting jeans and a very revealing matching blouse. And try as I might, to keep my eyes off her, she tried twice as hard to make me notice her.

And I did notice her.

I also managed to spill my drink twice and I knocked my dish completely off the table, sending my veggies flying across her immaculate kitchen floor.

While her husband seemed amused by my actions, I had the feeling I was playing right into their hands.

Her husband seemed not to notice that when she was cleaning up my mess on her hands and knees, she kept brushing up against me and bending over right in front of me.

To me it became increasingly apparent that the woman was more than flirting with me. She was making a play for me. And it was obvious her husband approved of all this.

After my mess had been cleaned up she came around the table to serve me everything again.

This was something she had never done before.

Of course, none of us had ever acted this way before either.

Or was this all just in my mind?

And when she 'accidentally' bumped against me hard, feigning a stumble on the carpet, I almost jumped out of my chair!

Was that bump intentional?

To get a reaction?

Then I realized that her husband had been studying me throughout this charade.

At first I had thought that my feeling of uneasiness was because I had done something wrong.

But now that the game was in play, I somehow felt that my boss and the woman wanted to say something, but they didn't know what to say, or they were afraid to start the conversation.

This new realization made me even more uncomfortable, and I suddenly wanted to quickly finish my meal and go back to work.

I had never been much for small talk.

I had been taught to only speak when I was asked a question and to ask a question when I wanted to know something or I wanted something.

After all, I was only 16 years old, and in my culture I had no right to question those older than me, but then again, this only applied to my People.

I wanted to get out of their presence so badly.

I wolfed down the food on my dinner plate, then I excused myself and went back to work.

I almost ran from the main house as I made my way back to the safety of the barn and corrals.

Standing just inside the barn trying to catch my breath, the full realization of what had just happened hit me.

"Oh God!"

"She."

"No."

"They."

"They want me to be the father of her child."

My mind was racing.

"Oh God!"

I prayed for Bobby again.

I prayed for me.

I prayed for them.

I prayed for me again.

Then I thought,

"What the hell is wrong with me? Am I that stupid? I'm young. I've never been with a woman before. What makes me think they would want me to do anything like that? I gotta be crazy to think anything like that. I'm tired and I miss my friend, and I'm angry about what happened to him, that's all."

But now, even as I worked twice as hard, I dreaded suppertime.

During dinner, neither of them had mentioned Bobby, although they'd heard about it on the radio while we were eating.

The woman did ask if I knew that poor boy, and I had only nodded that I had.

I knew I had to stop thinking about Bobby and that woman, so I tried to put my mind to rest with another prayer for strength and guidance, and to say a final good bye to my friend. Then I focused on the work at hand.

The first day had passed mostly uneventful except for what had happened at dinner.

I knew that my spirit was having an inner conflict I had not known before.

I was tired when I had arrived here this morning, but I had worked hard and tried to stay focused on what I had to do.

During supper the boss and his wife seemed like their old selves and everything was pretty much what I used to know as normal. She had dressed down and we were all nice and polite, but after supper, they seemed to try extra hard to keep me in their house.

I felt they were at the brink of saying to me what they wanted to say, but this made me a little afraid and anxious. So I excused myself and I went back to the bunk house and took a shower.

I said my evening prayers and after a few hours of tossing and turning I finally fell asleep.

I had already been working for three hours when the lights in the main house came on.

Now it was early afternoon of the second day after I'd arrived and I was all done with what they had wanted me to do.

They had wanted me to clean out the barns and the corrals and spread the manure around in the fields.

Earlier that morning during breakfast, the tension of the night before seemed to be almost non-existent. This was more to my liking, and I went about my work more intently.

During dinner I had told the boss I would be done with my work in another hour or two, and that I wanted to go home, and they both had agreed we would leave right after supper.

Now that I was finished with my work, I went around to check on their other vehicles. There was still a few hours until suppertime, so I wanted to keep busy.

I changed a few tires that didn't look good, then I refilled all the fluids in the other vehicles, and I changed the oil and oil filter on her pickup truck.

When I had done that, I checked the air pressure in all the remaining vehicle tires as well.

Now as I was refueling the last of their vehicles, I remembered one of my uncles telling me,

"When you work for someone, act like you are working for God himself. Anything you can find that needs getting done, do it. Don't wait for someone to tell you. This is what will set you apart from a good worker. You will be a man that everyone wants. You will never be out of a job, because good is never good enough. You remember that."

I loved working for other people.

I knew my way around a farm and ranch. And this kind of work gave me independence. While I worked I had plenty of time to think and plan for my own future.

I was always ready and willing to help any of my many relatives with their work, but when I worked for them, it had to be labor of love.

Here working for these people and others like them, I was doing what I enjoyed doing, and I was supporting myself.

With what I earned I bought my own school clothes, and I could help grandma with things she wanted but didn't want to ask grandpa for.

Now that I had finished my work for these folks, I was going to take a nice hot shower and get ready for supper.

While I was repacking my bag, I thought that these folks needed a full time ranch hand around.

Sometimes things were just too much for a woman to handle alone, but I also felt that ranch hand couldn't be me.

What they needed was an older man, someone older than I am.

Someone with experience so he would do what had to be done without being told everyday what to do.

There was a lot of danger around a farm if one didn't pay attention.

Then I thought about my boss again, and I could feel that small anger moving around in my stomach again.

I wondered what had the boss been thinking about when the accident had happened?

I remembered that another of my uncles had told me,

"You have to have respect when you work. Respect your tools. Keep them clean, polished and dry. Keep them sharp if they need sharpening. Keep them oiled if they need oil, and keep your vehicles ready to go. Pay attention to what you are doing at all times. When you don't respect your work or your tools, accidents are no accident. Things will happen."

After I had taken my shower and I had put on clean clothes, I went and parked the woman's pickup truck back where she usually parked it. Then I went into their house to wait for supper.

As far as I knew, I was finished here and I felt light and happy, knowing I would be home in a few hours.

But during supper, when they tried to make small talk again, everything seemed forced, nothing seemed to work.

This time the clumsiness was not mine.

I just sat and watched and listened.

What was happening?

The thought of a child almost entered my head again, but I pushed that aside and quietly ate my supper.

When I came to work for them before, small talk usually came easy for them.

But this time, something was definitely wrong.

I knew they could feel it as well.

I just wished they would come out and say whatever it was they had to say.

I couldn't take the tension any longer, so I told them I would be waiting in the bunkhouse when they were ready to take me home.

Then I excused myself and I went outside.

I hadn't finished eating supper, but I could always eat something once I was back home.

I was suddenly very tired, so I went into the bunk house and lay down for a short nap, leaving the door open for circulation.

I must have been more tired than I had thought, because when I came awake, it was getting dark outside.

Something had awakened me, and I was just about to turn the light on when there was a light knock on the door.

"Come in."

I don't know how long she had been standing there, but when she realized that I was awake, she had knocked on the open door.

The woman didn't enter the room, but she stood there in the open door.

The room was dark, and with the yard light at her back, I could see the silhouette of her body through the thin material of her dress.

I was instantly embarrassed, yet I didn't turn on the light.

"What if she can read my thoughts?"

There are some people who can read people's minds, grandpa could, everyone knew that!

She didn't say anything, she just stood there with her back to the light, so I asked.

"Is anything the matter? Is something wrong?"

Then she took a step back and cleared her throat.

"I, I'm sorry,"

"Can I talk to you? Can we talk to you?" she stammered.

"Why certainly, just a second, I'll be right there, is everything okay? Is anything wrong? Is your husband okay?"

I reached to turn on the light and when I turned back towards the door, she was gone.

Her voice had seemed urgent, but she left without answering so I put on my boots and followed her out the door.

When I entered the kitchen she was sitting at the dinner table in her usual place.

She had her back to the living room where I knew her husband was sitting in the dark facing the wall.

"Please come in and have a seat."

"Do you want anything to drink?"

"Coffee or a soda?"

"No thank you. I'm fine. Is everything alright?"

I was surprised at how calm my voice was. I must have appeared completely composed, but that's not how I felt inside after seeing her in her see through night clothes.

I had come in through the back door, and I had remained standing with my back pressed to the door. My hands were clinched tightly around the door knob.

I was ready to flee.

After a short pause she regained her composure.

She took a deep breath, and at first she spoke softly while looking down into her lap where she had her hands folded.

As she spoke her confidence grew, and when we made eye contact, I could see her fear and feel her anxiety, yet I knew that she really wasn't afraid of me.

"I, I don't know how to begin to do this."

"I don't know what to say."

"But my husband and I have talked about this for a long time, and at great length."

"And he thought, he thought I should be the one to ask you."

Now she put her folded hands on the table in front of her, glancing back into the living room as she continued,

"As you probably know by now, we can't possibly have any children. I mean, after the accident. My husband can't. You know? But we want to have a baby. I want to have a baby."

With this first part of what she had to say finally out in the open, she no longer had any fear or anxiety in her voice, or her eyes.

"We needed to, wanted to find someone with dark features. We needed to find someone who was tall like my husband, with dark hair and dark eyes. We needed someone who looks like us. We needed someone who is good looking, someone who comes from a good family and someone who has a good family background."

She paused here long enough to let her words sink in, then she said, "You fit that bill."

And with that said, she took a deep breath and let out a sigh.

All the tension that had filled the last two days, had now been released.

But I felt like I had just been kicked in the stomach.

I wanted to run!

To escape!

After her husband had heard his wife finish addressing me, he turned his wheelchair around and I could clearly see that the uneasiness had gone from him as well.

The question was out, and they were both relieved to have gotten the question out.

Now it was up to me.

What would my answer be?

"I'll have that cup of coffee now if you don't mind."

As I slowly took my usual place at the table I said,

"I'll need some time to think about this. I'll need time to...," but I couldn't finish my sentence.

Her husband had wheeled himself to his usual place at the kitchen table, and now he sat looking at me, checking my facial features, looking right into my very soul.

51

As her words sank in, I could feel myself flush.

The palms of my hands were sweaty.

I could feel my body temperature rising.

I was growing increasingly hot sweaty and very uncomfortable.

"What was happening?"

When she brought my coffee and set it down in front of me, without thinking I picked it up and drank it down in one big gulp.

Ouch!

Hot!

I was shaken.

My soul was shaken.

I had to think about this.

No! I didn't want to think about this.

"Grandma, help me!"

My mind raced.

That was it!

I had read about something like this with grandma.

It happened in a story from the Bible.

It turned out that the woman who had asked her handmaiden to do this exact same thing with her husband, hated her after it was over, to the point that she even tried to have her killed.

"So now what?"

Seeing my mounting despair over what they'd just asked of me, her husband broke in,

"Please don't think that we haven't talked about this."

"We have."

"We both know what we want."

"You wouldn't have to do anything except, you know."

I sat in unmoving silence.

I already felt guilty.

As if I had already done the deed and I was just now being found out.

My mind was racing.

I could hear the blood rushing in my ears.

I had to get away and think about this.

No! I didn't want to think about it!

I didn't want to think about anything.

I just wanted to get away, now!

I had to get away, I had to talk to grandma.

Then her husband continued,

"No one else would have to know."

"We would want it that way. No one would have to know."

"And the baby, he or she, would be ours."

Now they were both sitting there staring at me, then they would glance hopefully at each other, leaning forward on the table, trying to coax an answer out of me.

All the while my discomfort and my uneasiness was starting to show more.

Suddenly they both seemed very calm.

They had their hands folded on the table top, now they were holding hands, resigned to the idea, knowing full well that I would agree.

Knowing I would jump at this idea.

After all, who would turn down a chance to be with a beautiful woman?

Who in their right mind would turn down a chance like that?

Sensing my desperation, the woman said,

"We've been looking, searching for someone for a long time now. We would hire someone who would seem like someone we would want, but somehow, they've never worked out. There was always something about them that has always been wrong."

"Then we met you and your folks, your family. And we knew you were the one."

I had been looking down into my empty coffee cup, I was unable to meet their eyes.

Then she pleaded,

"Please."

"You don't have to make a decision right now. We still have a day or two. I'll be in my cycle by then."

"If you want anything. I mean, we know you work for everyone around here. Everyone knows that your work is good. Everyone knows that you are a good man. We know you don't have a car, we could..." and she broke off her sentence, perhaps feeling my own mounting despair.

Then her husband made an offering,

"If there's anything we can do for you just let us know. If your family needs something, anything, just let us know."

I had been sitting with both hands wrapped around the coffee cup in front of me on the kitchen table.

The woman had gotten up and she was pouring me another cup of coffee when she leaned forward and pushed her breast hard against me.

The feeling of her moving against me almost made me explode, and she had caught that.

It had been intentional.

The last two days had been entirely intentional.

I had a tight feeling in my chest, I couldn't breathe, I wanted to get up and run away.

Feeling my urge to flee the wife made one last effort,

"We are running out of time. We want to do this while we are still young enough to raise a child."

"I mean, if you want too?"

"We'll do this only if you want too."

"You can take more time to think about this if you want?"

"If you want?" she pleaded.

I didn't drink that last cup of coffee.

Instead, I pushed myself away from the table and got slowly to my feet.

I was lightheaded, dizzy, so I leaned on the table to steady myself.

I didn't bother to excuse myself, I knew I wouldn't be able to speak yet in my natural voice. But as I pulled the door closed, I could hear her say,

"See you at breakfast then?"

I only nodded as I made my way out the door.

When I was outside, for the first time, the entire farm yard looked alien to me in the bright moon light.

"What was that?"

"What had just happened?"

"Naw! It had to be a dream."

As I stood looking at the stars, I said a silent prayer, then I went back inside the bunkhouse and closed the door.

I waited an extra hour after the lights had gone off in the big farm house, before I picked up my bag and tiptoed out of the yard, feeling like a thief stealing away into the night.

When I was out of the driveway and out onto the road I opened her up to a full gallop.

I ran full out until I couldn't see the lights from the farm anymore, then I slowed my pace to an easy jog.

When I was sure I wasn't being followed, I slowed to a more relaxed gait.

As I walked along I thought about the last few days events.

What had I done to deserve all this attention?

This late night run was clearing my mind and I felt good.

After a while my thoughts were back under control.

I knew I could never do what my friends had just asked of me to do.

Surely her husband would hate me eventually.

Just as that woman had hated her handmaiden in that story grandma had read. And just maybe her husband would eventually want to kill me too, who knows?

Or perhaps the wife might eventually want to leave her husband.

I didn't want to be any part of any of it.

I walked on, sometimes I would break into a run.

I already knew I would not go back to work for them, or ever see them again.

I knew that once you bare your heart to someone, like they had just done to me, and you get rejected, they would not feel kindly toward me ever.

I thought of my grandmother and I knew I would not tell her of what had just happened tonight.

It would be my secret.

Then I wondered what grandma would have for breakfast this morning.

"Good night grandma, I'll be seeing you in the morning."

A couple of hours before daylight I stopped to rest on one of the stone buttes that lines White Shirt Creek. I was only a few miles from home, yet I wasn't tired at all.

I knew this was from the adrenaline surge from the night I would never forget. And I would probably pay for this exertion later on tonight, but I was in pretty good shape, so I pushed on.

A few days after I had arrived home, my grandfather gave me a letter addressed to me. I waited until I was all alone, then I opened it.

Inside the envelope was a check for a full weeks work.

Also inside the envelope was a short note written in the woman's hand,

"Please don't feel badly towards us. We just saw something good and we wanted to have a small piece of that goodness. We know we will not see you again, but we will think often of you. We both wish you well."

…the note was unsigned.

YAMNI

After coming home under very different and unusual circumstances, I took a break. I stayed around the home place for a while working for my grandfather.

Grandpa had some hay that needed to get done so naturally, I volunteered. But after I was finished I got restless so I went back into town. I thought I might get on a haying crew with some of my uncles.

Working a haying crew with others was less money, since everyone would be paid by the bale. Depending on how many bales we could haul in a day, we would divide that by the number of men on the crew.

We usually stayed out a week at a time, leaving Sunday evening and coming back to town on Friday evening.

We would spend the weekend in town and go back out on Sunday evening. We would do this until the haying season was over.

Right now I didn't care how much I earned.

I just needed to be with some older men so I could listen to them tell their stories of long ago.

After I'd arrived in town, I went to spend the night at one of my other grandfathers'. And I let it be known at the local bar, that I was available for work if someone should need an extra hand on their crew.

Sure enough, on Sunday evening grandpa Maynard came looking.

Maynard was known far and wide to have one of the better work crews around the reservation, so I was glad when he came after me.

There were a lot of younger crews who competed for the haying contracts, and they did earn more because they worked a lot harder than these old guys.

But I preferred the company of these older men.

They made work fun and interesting. Many of the things I heard and learned while with these older guys was invaluable.

Most of the men on grandpa Maynard's crew had been together a long time. They always sought each other out when a farmer or a rancher needed more than one hand. And during haying season they always worked together.

Besides, I was a good listener and I enjoyed the stories of long ago, even if I'd heard them already, it still was a treat.

We had been out a week now, working for a man out by Morristown. The work had been uneventful, except that one time during the week, when the boss had asked the men about the sun dance and everyone got up and had walked out on supper.

Now it was Friday, early evening and our haying crew had retired to the old loading dock behind Lawien's Hardware.

Everyone had ordered sandwiches from Swanson's Bar and Grill, and they each had their own preference of drinks.

I had ordered extra cheese burgers and cokes and I followed them into the loading dock, making my bedroll on the dock. The other men made their bedrolls in a circle, head to feet, below me on the ground.

Up here I could hear everything without any distraction.

They were all single men, in their early thirties to late forties. They were all veterans of the different branches of service and the different wars. And although I wasn't related to any of them through blood, I was related to a few of them by a previous marriage.

Uncle Wimpy, had lived with one of my aunts from time to time. This man could fix anything, operate anything, and he was a top ranch hand. He actively rode at local rodeos representing the ranch he was working for at the time.

Daddy Stan, was once married to my mother and they had one daughter. This man was a good farm and ranch worker. He was quiet, but he was a thinker. He usually spoke last after everyone else had spoken their thoughts. But he liked to play devil's advocate, and ask questions that would get the other men to respond.

Uncle Jake, had two children with one of my aunts and their marriage had lasted just as long. This man was steeped in Lakota Culture. He was a singer for the people, however, sometimes going astray. But he knew all the songs and tribal customs, and sometimes late in the evening he would sing those songs.

Grandpa Maynard, was probably the most colorful of the bunch. He certainly was the oldest, and in my eyes he could do no wrong. He had the most wisdom and he also actively rode in local rodeos, just like uncle Wimpy.

I had been looking forward to this weekend.

Because of what had happened at supper that one night after work, I just knew that daddy Stan wouldn't let this one slide.

Sometime during the week at supper time, the boss had mentioned that while he was in town, he had stopped at the bar to have a beer and pick up on the latest news.

While he was having his beer, he said this young Indian man had asked him to buy him a drink, which he did.

In conversation he learned the young man was on his way to a sun dance. Apparently the young man had been sun dancing for a few years. I guess he had taken off his shirt to show the boss his scars to prove it.

Then he asked our boss to buy him another drink, which he did.

The boss wanted to know more about the sun dance, so at supper that night after work, he asked the men if they knew anything about it.

When the boss had asked, all the men had stopped eating. I didn't know what to do, so I stopped eating too.

When the boss asked what was wrong, no one said anything, but the men all sat with their heads down, so I sat with my head down too.

When the boss asked a second time about the sun dance, grandpa Maynard said that it was not to be discussed, then the men started eating again, so I started eating too.

When the boss asked why not, grandpa Maynard excused himself and walked out of the house.

All the men followed close behind him, and since I didn't know what to do, I followed them all out the door.

I had followed them out the door, except I didn't know why no one wanted to share anything with the boss.

They usually told him whatever he wanted to know about the Lakota.

Usually.

As I was settling in for the night, I knew this was going to be the topic for this evening, and I wouldn't miss it for the world.

When everyone was settled, the men rolled smokes and sat smoking quietly, passing one of their bottles around, but no one was saying a word.

Finally, daddy Stan opened up one of his bottles and took a nip, then he handed it to uncle Wimpy, then he asked,

"Well, what do you boys think? Shall we talk about it? Or shall we leave it alone?"

The men just sat quietly smoking and passing their bottles around, as if no one had heard the challenge.

Uncle Wimpy took a drink and passed the bottle around, then he said,

"No. I don't want to talk about it."

"All I will say is that it's wrong. It's wrong in what that young man was doing. He is fooling with something he knows nothing about."

Although no one made a noise, I could tell they all agreed that it was wrong.

Neither grandpa Maynard nor uncle Jake said a word.

They just passed the bottles around and sat quietly, so daddy Stan said,

"Okay, let's look at it from that angle. What do you boys think? If it's wrong, what will become of that young man?"

The response was quick and the voice was a little angry.

"You all know that the sun dance is not for everyone, and that you must live in a certain way?, and that this thing is not to be taken lightly."

It was uncle Jake.

He was sitting with his back to the wall and he had his eyes closed, but he continued,

"And you ask. What will become of that young man? What do you think he is afraid of? For surely what is in his heart will come to pass. And if not on him, then on those he loves. But maybe on him and on all those he loves too. You just don't know."

Again there was general agreement, but you could tell uncle Wimpy was getting agitated too, because he opened up with,

60

"First of all, how many of you have sun danced before? None of you? I know why none of you sun dance. It's because you have blood on your hands. Since you have come home from war, none of you have been to the cleansing ceremony to get clean. Now you want to talk about the sun dance? Huh!"

And with that, uncle Wimpy snorted and took a long pull on one of the bottles. And although he didn't smoke, he rolled one and lit it up, then he handed it to grandpa Maynard.

Grandpa Maynard took the offered cigarette, cleared his throat, then he said very deliberately,

"I know that the young men are not allowed to sun dance every year as this young man does, and I know that this is what our young ones are trying to do now. They are not dancing as in the old way. They are trying to dance for themselves, for show, and for money."

Then he took a long drag on his smoke and he took a drink from his bottle while the others sat watching. Then he took another drag and let the smoke out slowly, then he continued,

"I know that a man, in his life time, has only three chances at the sun dance, and that is twelve years. And I know that if his prayer is not answered in all his dancing, then that is all. He is finished. He is not allowed to dance ever again. That is all."

Uncle Jake broke in here,

"We cannot discuss this thing at length, but we can talk about it in general, is that agreeable?"

Again, all the men were in agreement, so he continued.

"Well then, if it's okay with you all, I will tell you what must be done to have a sun dance."

Two of the men got up to relieve themselves and when everyone got settled again, uncle Jake continued.

"First. The sun dance is not for everyone. Only the men can sun dance. But before one can sun dance, one must prepare for four years. He must have a reason to dance, and it cannot be a selfish reason. His request must be for the People, to help them in some way. Then after he makes preparations, he can dance."

"After everyone is pierced, then the dance is started. There are no breaks for food or water. This is a dance of sacrifice. The dancer is to suffer for the People. He must be sincere in his prayers."

"Now, the very first dancer whose piercing have been pulled through, his prayers have been answered. The dance is finished. No matter how many others are dancing or no matter how many others have not had their piercing pulled through. The dance is finished. The others, if they wish to dance again, they must wait for four more years. And they must be pure. Only if they are pure can they dance again. They only have three chances to ask and have their prayers answered, after that, they can dance no more, does everyone understand?"

After uncle Jake had finished, no one questioned the discussion. It was laid out plain for them. Only the bad part had to be answered yet.

But the men had gotten stiff from sitting around and they decided to go for a walk along the railroad tracks.

Only I remained behind.

It was late when the men returned and it was plain that they had been discussing the other questions concerning the bad part of the sun dance.

I knew that the ending for the story would be retold just for me, so I would not fall into the trap of trading my culture for money, just as that young man was doing. The young man whom their boss had met at the bar.

After the men had reseated themselves and had gotten comfortable, uncle Jake asked grandpa Maynard to tell what he had heard some years ago.

It went like this...

"It seems a family, a man and his woman and their three kids had been putting on a show for some white people in town. Something they should not have been doing because it was for money."

"It seems the man got it in his head that money made him equal with the white man. But the only way he could make a lot of money was to show off in front of the white man. It also seems that the white man is curious and he will pay for what he doesn't know. And it seems that if you make it mysterious and more magical, the white man will pay more."

"Anyway, they say that the man and his family lived in an old cavalry tent, a square tent with straight walls. The kind which has to be tied down. It seems this man was not only greedy, but he was lazy as well, so he put his tent up beside a barbed wire fence."

"They say that he had never seen a barbed wire fence before, but he put his tent there because the posts were already up and they were very sturdy, so he tied his tent up to the fence posts, and he also tied up some of the tent ties to the wire itself."

"They say the man and his family had been living there in their tent for a few weeks, then one day they could see the storm brewing."

"They say that these storm clouds were much darker and had more lightening than other storms anyone had ever seen before, and maybe they said that as a sign of what was to happen."

"Anyway, they say that when the wind and the rain hit, the tent stood up against them, because the posts that it was tied too were very strong and they were put in the ground very deep."

"They say that while the man was boasting to his wife and his sons about what a smart man he was, a bolt of lightening hit the barbed wire fence someplace, and because lightening has to go into the ground, they say the lightening traveled along the barbed wire fence until it came to the tent with the people inside, then it went into the ground."

"They say that the people in the tent were all found dead by some people from the town who had came to ask the man to tell his stories and do his magic again. But they had all been killed by the lightening, because the tent was wet, and lightening is attracted to heat and must be grounded, and what could be more grounded than five people in a wet tent that is tied to a barbed wire fence in an electrical storm?"

Grandpa Maynard was getting himself angrier with the retelling of this story.

He finished it with,

"And what do you think that man was afraid of?"

No one bothered to answer.

All through the telling of this last story, the men had been very still. No one moved, not even to take a drink or roll a smoke. Now that the story was ended, the small circle was a scene of activity.

Everyone was rolling out their bed rolls, or rolling their last smokes, or taking that last drink before they turned in.

I sat eating one of my burgers thinking about what had just happened.

I could see the story unfold as if I had been there to witness it all.

When I was finished eating, I jumped off the loading dock and I also took a short walk.

As I said my prayers that night, I remembered the man in the story and his family. Then I made up my bed roll and as I went off to sleep, I noticed that the others were already snoring.

Hau!

CEKPA

From the Author

One day when I was about 11 years old, my grandfather's niece had a set of twin boys. After that, every time we went to visit, my grandfather would make it a point to stop and see these boys.

Even when they were babies in their cribs, he would ask "Which is the good one and which is the bad one?"

Then he would chuckle to himself.

As the twins got older he would ask them, "Are you the good twin or the bad twin?"

Not knowing why he was asking them, I always took it as a form of teasing, until my grandmother related this story to me.

The question that brought out the Cekpa story was simply, "Why can't people ever get along?"

I had asked it during a time of stress, under my breath, not knowing that she or anyone else had been listening.

But this ritual with my grandfather continued until his death in the mid 1980's.

In our story, even though the Creator hadn't meant to harm his children, in a round about way that has happened.

Today we find we are ultimately responsible for our decisions, or even our indecisions. We have become creators of our own destiny, and we must teach our children that although the choices we make today may not affect us today, somewhere down the road, each choice we make today will affect us or those we come into contact with sometime down the line. Maybe not today, tomorrow or even this week, but certainly there will be a consequence for what we decide today.

Our children should know, that our choices are very important, no matter how insignificant those choices may seem when they are made.

Also in our story, before the arrival of the twins, the people lived in harmony. They worked together, they played together, and they worshipped together.

After the twins departed, then the dissention and the doubt came to live with the People. Quite possibly, the very worst seed that was planted was gossip and rumor.

We've all seen what gossip and rumor have done to our families, our villages, and our Nations.

And now "Cekpa" which is Lakota for "umbilical cord", "the navel" and also meaning "twins."

Hau!
(for Mark and Mike)

CEKPA

(The Twins...)
A Short Story
by
Eya Mani

Long long ago before the coming of the white man, the Lakota lived in peace.

The Creator provided enough wild game for hides for their shelter and for their clothing, and they had plenty of meat and a variety of small game and game birds and fish.

With wild fruit and roots and herbs they dug up and harvested during the seasons, they had a variety of foods, more than enough to live well, and also to provide for their medicines.

The People were happy and content and they spent much of their time playing, or as one would say today, they loved to pow-wow.

The People would give thanks to the creator for their good fortune, then they would sing songs and dance, and their children would play games and the men would gamble.

The younger women also would compare their work to see who among them had made the finest quill work and who had made the brightest colors.

And the older women would compare their work to see who had made the finest and strongest stitches, and who among them had made the very finest of tanned hides.

All this was done with good intent, and because the People had such a good way of life, they started the practice of giving the very finest they had to the first person who admired their work.

And this free will giving too was done in reverence to the Creator and to mother earth and to the many animals and plants that had sacrificed themselves so their work would be complete and admired by all.

Now, it is said that one day the Creator was admiring his children and he was discussing their good nature and attitude with mother earth, and because the Creator likes a good joke, he wanted to play one on his children.

But mother earth was not so keen about letting the Creator play jokes on her children.

But he persisted so after a time she finally consented and told him that he could play one joke on them.

However, she made him promise that he would not harm her children because they had such a respect for her and such reverence and regard for him.

After much thought and in consideration of her request, he said he would send them a present.

He told her that his present to the People would be the ability to choose their own destiny. To have the ability to choose right from wrong and to make their own choices as to which of these roads they would follow.

When mother earth heard this, she also made him promise that he would leave all decision making totally up to their children, and he would not interfere with their right to decide.

And so it was.

As his instrument, the Creator made his first set of twins.

Of course these were not ordinary twins, they were very special twins. And to help them with his joke, the Creator had given them special magical powers.

And although they appeared normal in everyway, there was a difference between the two.

They were made the exact opposite of each other.

While one was good, kind and generous, the other was not so good, kind or generous.

One might say the one twin was contrary, which almost means naughty or mischievous. And although he was not bad, because no one knew what bad was yet, one might even say that he was adventurous, because he was always looking for new ways to bring attention on himself, and he would find it anyway he could.

When mother earth had observed the twins long enough to see that they would not harm her children, she told the Creator that it was time to play his joke.

And with that, the twins were set loose.

The twins were told to go out and "move among the People."

But they were not to become involved with the People directly or harm the People in any way.

They were only to create situations and circumstances where the People would have to choose right from wrong.

And so, the twins set out on their first adventure.

As it happened the time was when the timpsila (wild turnups) are harvested, probably in mid-June.

During this time of the seasons, the People have a lot of work to do, and as you all know, when People are at work, they don't like to be bothered.

After observing the People at work and after making plans, the twins blew themselves in on a western wind.

They had taken the form of two large tumbleweeds, and they had created a wind which blew them towards a group of tipi's which were standing along a beautiful river valley, and again they stopped and watched the People working.

After a time, the contrary twin said he would be first and he demanded the good twin go along with him on this first encounter.

After a short discussion, the good twin finally agreed, and so the contrary twin took the form of an old man and the good twin was made into an old woman.

The old woman was placed upon an old broken down sway back horse and the old man was leading the horse.

All were in very bad condition and when the People saw them approaching, they could clearly see that these two very old and worn out travelers had seen some very hard times.

When the People saw them approaching, they immediately stopped work and gathered around.

A place was prepared for their guests and a meal was set for them. While still others got out their finest clothing and still others went to fetch their finest horses as gifts for these, their two impoverished guests.

After their visitors had eaten their fill and had rested, they were given food and the gifts from the People.

As the old man and old woman were preparing to leave, they were asked where they had come from and where they were going.

The contrary twin, who had taken the form of the old man, knowing of the peoples love to sing and dance, told them that they had heard that there was to be a big celebration at such and such a place, and that they had come a very great distance to attend.

The People were also told that everyone was invited to attend because this celebration was to be very big and impressive, with the playing of many games, there would be much gambling, and everyone was assured that they would all enjoy themselves should they decide to attend.

As the old man and old woman were in a hurry to spread the word to all those they encountered, and also to get a good camp ground, they left soon after.

After the old couple had gone, the People went back to work giving little thought to what they had been told by the old man.

But some, mostly the younger ones, were impressed with the news of the "big doings" and they wanted to attend, and some even went so far as to start making preparations to leave camp, thus disrupting the timpsila harvest.

To settle this issue, the camp leader sent out a rider to go ask their relatives who were also camped out down stream along the river a few miles away, to ask what their intent was.

The rider returned and said that their brothers down stream had also received a visit from these two old People.

He reported that when they had come into the village, they also had been in very bad condition and he wondered what had become of the fine clothing, food, goods and horses that the People had given to them as gifts?

The rider also reported that there was now dissention in camp, because the younger folks wanted to attend this big doings at such and such a place. And that their work there too had been disrupted.

Since the time of the big doings was a few days off, the two camp leaders decided to meet and discuss what their people wanted to do.

Meanwhile they sent riders to the other camps along the river to bring word back about what the People were going to do about the big doings.

On the appointed day of the celebration, two riders were again sent out, this time to track the old couple.

On the appointed day of the celebration, two riders were again sent out, this time to track the old couple.

When the two riders returned from tracking the old couple to the supposed celebration camp site, the story they told was both astonishing and comical.

It seems that when the two riders had approached the site of the celebration, they couldn't see anyone around, but they could hear two voices, so they approached unseen.

The riders said that two individuals were having an argument, but when the riders crept closer to hear what was being said, all they saw was two rather large tumbleweeds, and the voices seemed to be coming from them.

And they said the two voices seemed to be in an increasingly heated argument, with one voice taking the lead and scolding the other voice.

Then right before their eyes, the two tumbleweeds were changed into two identical twins.

These were the first twins the two riders had ever seen, and they didn't know what to think of it!

The contrary twin was walking around in circles with his hands behind his back, once in awhile he would stop and gesture wildly with his hands.

But he continued to complain that the good twin had not been convincing enough to fool the People into believing that there indeed would be a pow wow.

And all the while, the good twin seemed to not pay any attention to him.

Instead, he was seated on the ground surrounded by all the goods given to them by the People and he would make a comment or two about the generosity of the People.

Then he unpacked some of the food they had been given and he ate some and he even offered some to the other twin.

But the contrary twin continued to pace back and forth scolding the good twin.

Finally the good twin unpacked some goods and was now admiring the tanned hides, with their straight strong stitches and the bright colors of the quill work, and this angered the contrary twin even more and he stopped pacing and he threw some dust into the air.

Then he told the good twin that because of him they had missed a chance to have a really good laugh, if everyone had shown up as he had expected.

He went on to comment that the people would have been very angry and confused, and they would have started pointing fingers and arguing, and this and that.

Then he openly tried to get an argument out of the good twin.

But the good twin only offered the contrary twin something else to eat as he himself finished off another portion of dried meats sweetened with wild fruits.

The contrary twin threw his hands up and flopped him self down in the dirt in disgust.

When he had had his fill, the good twin commented that they should be on their way since no one was going to show up and be fooled.

Without another word, the twins turned themselves into tumbleweeds and although there was no breeze blowing, they "blew" themselves down the river bank, across the waters, and up the opposite river bank and they rolled on out of sight.

After hearing this tale of magic, the People sat and wondered.

But many doubted.

And whether the story is true or not, there is one thing you can be sure of.

The People were no longer happy and content as they once had been, because the twins had planted the seeds of dissent, doubt, and gossip.

So beware, the next time you see two large tumbleweeds on the move, know that the twins have been visiting, and only time will tell what fruits their work will bear.

Hau!
(for Mark and Mike)

THE MEANING OF THE TIPI POLES

(from the Author)

From my earliest childhood memories, we have always been taught how to treat other people, in private and in public, and how we are to treat all things that we have been blessed with.

Because I am a tipi maker, I feel I must include this short story if only to associate those thoughts and beliefs that we hold so dearly, with our daily lives.

There is a book I've read that outlines those guidelines to better living, written by Joseph M. Marshall III, which he calls THE LAKOTA WAY.

In my discussion with Mr. Marshall about "the 12 Virtues of the Lakota" I asked him if the things written about in his book had been associated with the Tipestola, or the Tipi as we commonly call it today.

Upon hearing his answer, I decided that I would provide that story as it was presented to me.

There is a word that describes all that is Lakota, and that word is Wolakota.

After you have read my next offering, you will understand its meaning.

In my next offering I hope to strengthen those Virtues that Mr. Marshall has so forthrightly presented to us.

Hau!
(for my sons Justin, Tim and JR)

THE TIPI POLES

by

Eya Mani

One day I sat watching my grandfathers, my father and some of his brothers putting up a log house. They took great care in measuring, trimming and putting each log in place, making sure it fit just right.

Sometimes they would take it back out and reshape it, and refit it to make sure it would be strong and safe for whom ever was going to live in that house.

My grandmothers and aunts were making a large dinner for the workers and I was helping them by hauling water, getting them firewood and staying out of the way.

When my grandmother had unpacked a large roll of canvas and some long slim railings, I got curious because I had never seen anything like this before in my life.

When I asked her what she was doing, she smiled and laid out all the poles, stakes, ropes and the tipi cover, then she refolded it as if to repack it again.

When she had finished, she called me over and asked if I had seen how she had refolded it, and when I answered that I had, she started from the beginning and unpacked it and as she worked she told me this story.

"My grandson, we Lakota called our homes Tipestola, because of its shape. First we will take three tipi poles (Wahinpaspa) and tie them together here," and she marked each pole after she had measured it against the length of the folded tipi cover lying on the ground.

"Our tipestola is made up of a framework of 10 poles, and two poles will hold open the flaps at the top, bringing that number to 12. Each pole has a name, and just like the seasons, we have a name for each of them too."

"Our first three poles are named Honor (Wayuonihan) and it will stand on the south side. We will put Respect (Ahokipa) on the north side, and Humility (Unsiiciyapi) will be toward the east, but it will also be the south door pole" and as she talked she worked tying the poles together.

"These first three must be strong because it is on these three things that we will rest the other tipi poles, and our beliefs upon."

"Next we will put in the north door pole, and its name is Sacrifice (Icicupi). Next to that we will put in Love (Cante Ognake), next to that we will put in one more, its name is Truth (Wowicake), now we will put next to the south door pole Wisdom (Woksape), and next to that we will put in Perseverance (Wowacintanka), and in the back we will put in Compassion (Waunsilapi)."

"Next we will take another strong pole, and name this one Fortitude (Cantewasake), it will hold up our tipestola cover so we can finish. It must be tied here, and the tie must be strong so our tipestola will stand for as long as we will need it."

"Now we must first bind the nine standing poles together," and with that she walked around the framework tightening and retightening the rope, until she was satisfied that it was good.

My grandmother left me then to help with the meal, but she told me to study it and try to remember what I had just been told and what I had just seen her do.

As I stood looking at the standing framework and tried to memorize the names for each pole, one of my grandfathers took a water break and came to where I was standing. He put his hand on my shoulder and asked me if I knew why we named each tipi pole and why there were only ten in the framework.

"I think grandpa, it's because we must have all these things to live by. We must care for each other and have respect for others, and we must love and honor one another and we must be strong and brave."

"Yes, that's true" he answered as he offered me a drink from his dipper of water.

"But the most important thing to remember is that the tipi, our home, belongs to the woman. As long as we have these things in our hearts and as long as we live by them, we will always be welcome into her house. If we don't have these things in our hearts, and if we don't live by these things, the woman can kick us out of her house. Then we must leave her place until such time as we can live by what her house is made of."

He spilled the remaining contents of the dipper on the ground and wiped his mouth with his sleeve, then he asked me.

"Do you understand?"

"Yes grandfather."

"Now, which tipi pole is the most important do you think?"

After I didn't answer him, he said,

"Think about that one, and when you know, come and tell me."

After the men had eaten and had gone back to work, the rest of us had dinner. I could not eat so I asked my grandmother which tipi pole was the most important to her.

Instead of answering me, she asked me what was most important to me. I didn't know what to say but I answered.

"I think its Humility and Sacrifice, because those are the two at the door, you must enter the tipi through them."

"You are both right and wrong. But this is the reason for being right and wrong. You cannot have one without the other, one cannot stand alone, each makes the others stronger, they each need one another to stand together. In naming our poles we remember how we are supposed to live each day. And if we live this way each day, and treat others in this manner, others will in turn treat us the same way."

We had walked back to the standing framework and she asked me.

"Now, what do you suppose the names of our last two tipi poles will be?"

I had no idea and I said so, so she continued.

"Those last two are named Bravery (Woohiteka) and Generosity (Canteyukan). Now remember, you must have the three first on which to lean the others. Do you remember which those are? Do you understand?"

I told her that I understood, and I hugged her real tight, then I went to eat my supper.

And with that, my lesson was done.

I had not forgotten to tell my grandfather what he had asked me, but I knew that he understood.

As I watched my grandmothers and aunts complete the setting up of the tipestola, and stake and tie it down, I was very pleased with what I had learned that day.

Hau!

TOKA WASTE KTE

From the Author

There has been much talk of the Lakota losing their culture.

This should not be allowed to happen.

Many of the "Old Ones" are leaving us now and it is up to us to make sure this does not happen.

One way to keep the culture alive is to continue the storytelling, and keep it as accurate as we can so as not to bastardize our culture, this is my greatest fear.

As in my next offering, the younger boy is heard to say, "Grandma knows everything, let's go ask grandma."

That is the way of the old ones.

They seldom offer anything, if you want to learn, you had to ask.

That is the reality of youth.

You can ask why without being validated, without fear of reprisal, and if you ask the right person, you will have the correct answer and the reasons for it being the right answer.

There are many ways to get a name.

But one never, never names themselves like the younger ones are doing today.

It is because they do not know that they are doing this.

Our Lakota names came from the People, and in keeping with the tradition that the name be earned, for whatever reason, my next offering is an illustration.

In our story the renaming of the Lakota Warrior came at midlife, when the earning of names usually took place when the men were still young, but his deeds and the compassion he offered the enemy at a most crucial time in his life, tells of the true character of the man.

In the telling of Lakota stories we do not dwell on the inner battles of conscience or personal anguish, but rather we will tell of these only to let the reader know that there is a real conflict of cultures as in the story of "The Deer Hunter" and "Iyo'hi."

And now I offer you, "Toka Waste Kte."

Hau!
(for my brother Joe)

TOKA WASTE KTE

A Short Story

by

Eya Mani

The two boys had spent the morning chopping wood for old man Sees the Bear, who lived behind their grandmothers log house. Then they went from log house to log house and hauled water in buckets from the well in the middle of the community.

No one told them to do it.

It was something they did willingly and it was enough when the old ones looked at them with approving eyes and a hint of a smile.

Now it was almost noon and they sat on the big hill behind the Episcopal Church and looked down on the village from the west.

The village was small and there wasn't much to see.

It was just a scattering of log houses and old Army tents along the creek which separated their village into east and west.

Everyone knew everyone, and everyone lived in harmony with everyone else.

On the east side of the creek, there was a store with a post office and it was just north of the road at the foot of the long hill leading into the village from the east.

A Catholic Church stood just south of the store, again at the foot of the hill just beneath the cemetery which was along the hillside.

The Congregational Church which stood in the west part of town was just east of their grandmother's place. There was the BIA School which went to the 6th grade and it was along the road that came down from the east and headed out of town to the northwest.

The younger of the two boys started naming all the people they had helped that morning.

Bears Rib, Sees the Bear, Grey Eagle, Knocks Him Down, Eagle Pipe, Cedar Boy, and their aunt who was married to a man named Kills Pretty Enemy.

Their naming of the people turned to "how do you think they got their names?"

Neither of them knew although the older boy always made up stories of gallantry in battle and brave deeds done by the men in these families which led to their being named, and the younger boy as usual, settled on that.

But he was intrigued.

How did the old ones get their names?

He would ask grandma.

Grandma knew everything, but you had to ask.

The two boys jumped up and raced down the hill and as usual, the older boy let the younger boy win.

The younger boy would mock protest although he too knew that it was a gesture and being the older boys little brother, this always made him feel good about having a big brother.

They ate breakfast in silence and when they were finished eating, they made sure the wood was cut and the water buckets were full.

Their grandmother had gone outside to start making papa from the mule deer buck hanging in the coolness from the shade.

The older boy had gone to play with the older boys and he would most likely be gone the rest of the day, but the younger boy always stayed close by grandma.

Today he would help her hang up the meat to dry after she had cut it into thin slices.

Preparing.

All the older folks always seemed to be preparing for the something, for the unforeseen events which would be forth coming.

The younger boy was only about 8 years old, and he had friends too. But he was content to spend his time with grandma and help her as much as he could.

Mostly because she always told him stories of long ago after they did their work.

They both worked in silence, and when grandma started humming her songs, he knew she was content.

When he couldn't hold his question any longer, he asked her, "Grandma, who named all these people? I mean, how did they get their names?"

She did not answer him immediately, instead she just glanced at him and smiled and she continued to cut up the meat and hum the song she always hummed when she was content with her work.

He was going to ask her again when she put down her knife and looked at him and smiled.

"Grandson, where does that come from?"

"Do you really want to know?"

"Come, sit down here and sharpen these knives for me, and when you are finished I will tell you."

She put a sharpening stone on the ground in front of him and she got up and went into the log house.

When the boy had finished sharpening the knives she had been using, his grandmother came out of the log house with some fried meat and sliced fresh bread on a plate and they ate lunch.

When they had finished eating she asked him, "Who do you want to know about?"

The boy was puzzled, because although he wanted to know how they had gotten their names, he had never really thought about whose name, so he said "Uncle Gilbert."

"How did he get his name?"

"That one." she said matter-of-factly.

Her voice trailed off, and the boy could see she was in deep thought as she picked up another piece of meat, then she set it aside and stared out towards the river which was to the west of their village.

She sat a few moments in thought and then she said,

"That one, it is a story of great pain."

"And great love."

His grandmother turned to look into his eyes to make sure he understood what she was about to tell him.

When it was clear to her that he was in earnest, she said "But you cannot have one without the other."

The young boy settled down and got comfortable.

Whenever his grandmother told him stories of long ago, he could close his eyes and he could see the story unfold before him, like those "moving pictures" the older kids got to go watch at the school every summer, only he didn't have to go anywhere, because he had grandma.

When he was comfortable and she was sure the story would not be interrupted, the story began.

"Your uncle got his name from his father, but it was one of his fathers that got that name from the People, or so it has been said."

"It all happened long ago, before the coming of the whites."

"It is said that among the young warriors of the People, there was a young man who was very well known and respected among them."

"It is said he did everything he could for the People, more than was expected of him, and all the fathers wanted him to choose one of their daughters to be his woman."

"But the young man chose no one to be his woman and he just continued and he made a name for himself among the other People also, and soon his name was known far and wide, even among our enemies, the Crow."

"It is said that one day he did choose a young woman to be his, but by now he was not so young, but nevertheless, he remained a great warrior among the People and his name continued to be spread among the other bands of the Lakota as well. One could not go where no one knew his name."

"But, as in all things, there must be bad if there is to be good, so it is said that one day when all the men were out of camp, the Crow had come and they had stolen some horses and they had also taken some women."

"And they took them all back into Crow country, which is far away."

"One of the women that they had taken was this great warrior's woman."

"It is said that when he had heard this, he left immediately to hunt down the Crow who had taken his woman. He didn't wait for anyone to go with him, but he went alone."

"It is said that when he found a Crow camp, he rode right in and he went boldly from lodge to lodge looking for his woman, but that he couldn't find her in any camp or lodge of the Crow."

"After many days he returned to the People, who had all thought her dead by now, because some time had passed now and it was another season."

"It is said that this great Lakota warrior spent most of his time alone now, and the people knew that he must be in very great pain, because he really cared for that woman."

"But he continued on and he took no other woman, and none of the fathers offered him their daughters because by now everyone knew he would take no other."

"His name continued to be spread far and wide, and in his loss his name was made even greater."

"Then one day it was heard from some travelers, that a Lakota woman was living with the Crow at such and such a place."

"It is said that when this Lakota warrior heard that, he left immediately, alone, and when he found that camp, he rode right into the Crow camp and stole that woman back."

"It is said that he rode into the camp with such fury that the Crow ran away thinking that the Lakota surely had come to kill the entire camp. They didn't know that it was only one man."

"It is said that the woman he brought back was not the same woman that was taken some years back."

"It is also said that when the Crow came after the woman again, that she went back willingly, and some will say that she even ran away to be with this Crow."

"It is said that she had two children from this Crow who had stolen her some years back and that was the reason why she had run away, to be with her children."

"This time the Lakota warrior did not follow."

"Instead he thought a very long time about all that had been done."

"But he had to do what he had to do, and so, one day he put on his finest clothing, and he took his finest horses, and he took all his weapons, and he went back again to the Crow camp."

"This time he did not ride boldly into the Crow camp as he had done before, but he rode in close and it is said that he told the woman, that if she came with him, and if she brought her children, then he would let the Crow live, and they would leave in peace."

"But the woman would not."

"And it is also said that the Crow warriors, thinking that this lone Lakota warrior who was surely dressed to die, would be an easy kill."

"And so the Crow mocked him, and made fun of him, and they taunted him, but the Lakota warrior did not pay them any mind."

"It is said that the Lakota warrior asked her a second time to bring the children and return with him to their own people, and he would leave the horses as an offering of peace, but again she would not."

"And it is said that she too also mocked him, and taunted him, and made fun of him, and laughed at him."

"It is said that when the Lakota warrior and his horses had heard what the Crow and the woman had said to him, the horses also knew what they had to do."

"Because now the horses were also getting furious and they started stomping their feet and were prancing around, and they were eager for the fight."

"It is said that the Lakota warrior rode in with such fury that the Crow became confused and afraid, and they started to run everywhere trying to escape."

"It is said that all the Crow warriors were killed quickly and with such a vengeance that only the woman, her two children, and the Crow who had stolen her were left alive."

"And again, it is said, the Lakota warrior asked her to come with him a third time, and to bring her children with her and he would let the Crow live. But in her anger and in her fear she would not."

"So finally, it is said that the Lakota warrior told her that if that was her choice, then she would be with the Crow forever, and he killed them both."

"The People say that he brought those two children back to live with him among his own People. They say that he raised them two boys as Lakota warriors, and that they also were very fine men, making their names known far and wide among the People."

"From that time on, the People called him, 'Kills Pretty Enemy' because his woman had been very fair and good to look upon. But when she had chosen the Crow over him, he had to do what he had to do."

With that, the story was finished.

His grandmother sat quietly a few moments staring down towards the river. Then she got up and went back into the log house.

The young boy sat in awed silence, replaying the scenes over and over again in his mind.

Then he got his bow and arrows and went to play with his friends.

He never said a word about this to anyone.

But maybe, he would share this with his brother, someday.

Hau!

INDIAN COUNTRY

(a hostile term meaning enemy territory, or reservation)

From the Author

In 1969 five of my family embarked on a journey unlike any other. What we were to experience would shape our lives and the lives of our friends, our acquaintances, our family, and our future generations.

Although at this writing in early March of 2006, only my brother and I remain as survivors.

In February of 1969 my cousin George and I enlisted in the United States Marine Corps, specifically to go and experience the war in Vietnam.

In May of 1969, after my cousin Owen and my uncle Conrad Lee graduated from High School, my brother Joseph left College, and they also enlisted in the Marine Corps.

My brother Joe, my uncle Conrad Lee, my cousin Owen, my cousin George and I were to experience "hell on earth."

George was shot twice, once in the hand and once in the shoulder, but he survived only to come home and be beaten to death by unknown assailants in 2004.

Conrad Lee was wounded once but he survived and was sent back to the front where he was killed in September of 1970 in the Ashau Valley we Marines called the Valley of Death.

I brought him home on September 5th. He was only 17 years old at that time.

George, Owen and I had all just turned 20 years old in July and August of that year.

My brother was the oldest of us all, at 21.

Although we did not know it at the time, we would all eventually become "Casualties of War" as would our family members and our wives and our children, and our grand children.

My experience has strengthened my faith in the Creator, but my body is suffering from the ravages of war.

Once, while standing security for my men as they filled the company's canteens with river water, I went upstream 50 meters from the detail and I squatted down and looked into the water as it drifted by, and I saw what appeared to be an oil slick on the muddy discolored water.

I got up and very quietly moved a little further up stream, and I walked up on some bodies bloated, floating in the water along the shore.

Oozing blackened bodies that were draining body fluids into the water.

When I returned to my men, I said nothing of this to them, but I made sure they put two Halizone tablets into each and every canteen we had filled, before handing them back out to their owners for drinking.

When I drank water from my canteens, I had to hold my breath, and I tried to think of better times.

Those of us who have experienced combat first hand relive these episodes on a nightly, sometimes on a daily basis, time and time again.

Stress and Depression can trigger episodes of behavior that our families will never get used to sharing.

My personal therapy is to stay away from conflict, arguments, politics, large crowds, crying or screaming babies, and loud sudden noises.

Now that I am able to write about some of my experience, I've also found that talking about it up to a certain point again, is therapeutic for me, though not all the time.

With the Lords help, I will be whole again.

Now I offer you "Indian Country."

Hau!

INDIAN COUNTRY

(Enemy Territory or an Indian Reservation)

A Short Story
by
Eya Mani

The young man had fallen into a shallow, troubled sleep again. Barely on the verge of consciousness, but he could still hear them blades rotating.

Whup, whup, whup.

"Why won't they stop?"

"I'm so very tired. I just want to go home now."

Whup, whup, whup.

"Why won't they let me go so I can go home now?"

"Grammaaaaa."

The huge rotors of the CH-53 beat the air, causing the huge aircraft to shudder while slowing its decent carrying the Marines into battle.

This young man lying here dying, had been the company's 2-8 radio operator. This was a military term meaning he was the Captain's personal radio operator and he was also the communications chief of the company.

They were coming in on the second '53 into a hot landing zone.

Seated right across the gangway was the Captain, the Company Commander. He had his head down and he was holding his steel pot in his hands, slowly rotating it.

The young man leaned forward and looked up and down the gangway to see how the men were doing.

Young.

Everyone was so young.

Quiet.

Everyone was so quiet.

On most insertions, the men could be heard bandying around their most recent sexual escapades with the local girls from the surrounding villages, or telling lude jokes.

But not today.

As the radioman looked into these other young faces, most returned the acknowledgement with a nod while others immediately started checking their gear and weapons.

For their youthful appearances, it was deceiving, because most of these men were seasoned veterans of numerous gun fights and village incursions.

Grim.

Everyone was looking very grim.

Usually only one "Bush Company" was allowed in the rear at any one time.

But his company, Golf Company 2nd Battalion 7th Marines, had been recalled earlier than expected.

They were to resupply with their sister company, Hotel 2/7 at Battalion Headquarters, Hill 56 LZ Baldy, I-Corps, in the Republic of Viet Nam.

The word was, both Hotel and Golf Companies were being sent back into what the men called "the Valley of Death" because of what was reported as a very large enemy sighting in the Ashau Valley.

They had been called out a day earlier than expected and the severity of the situation was compounded by the Battalion Chaplain's impromptu "Sacrament of the Last Rights" he was performing while the men were saddling-up.

Then the men were assigned and were loaded onto the choppers, and just in case, every man was issued extra ammunition, just in case.

The young man's body started making involuntarily jerking movements, causing him to momentarily come awake in panic and just as suddenly, he would fall back into his almost coma-like sleep.

He remembered the first time he had seen her.

It was after his family had moved home from Los Angeles and he was going into the third grade.

On his first day of school, there she was, standing there just staring at him. There was nothing special about her really. She was just a scrawny little skinny kid with really big eyes and her hair was thin.

He remembered her, mostly because he had felt sorry for her. It was because everyone made fun of her and his People had told him she was "no good" because she was a half-breed and she came from a "bad family."

But he was too young to know of such things so he stuck up for her.

He remembered he had gotten into a fist fight with a 5th grade boy because he had been teasing her and had made her cry.

So to make things right, he waited after school for the older kids to get out of school, then he whipped the 5th grade bully real good.

But she wasn't there to see him do it because she had already been chased home by some of the other kids.

But when everyone in the small village had heard what he had done, no one ever bothered her again, and she even gained some friends because of what he had done.

The huge aircraft shuddered and looking down, he saw a large mushroom like hole appear between his feet. When he looked up he could see the sky through the exit hole made in the ceiling.

The round had narrowly missed the hydraulic lines running the length of the aircraft.

What would have happened had he still been leaning forward?

After his fight with the 5th grader, even the 6th grade boys made room for him when he came around. And he was almost always chosen first when teams were playing.

And when he was playing, "she" was always there to cheer him and his team on.

She brought him pop and candy from her home. These were things she always had and they were things he seldom got.

Someone had told him it was because that's the way her parents were. They never had time for her but they gave her things.

It was probably their way to show their affection towards her.

These things he did know about.

As they grew older, she continued to follow him around, always making it a point to be next to him at any event they both were attending.

She had even made friends with his female cousins so she could be close to him.

One day he asked his uncle Ray about her and the way she treated him.

Uncle Ray simply said, "You're her hero, she feels safe around you. She trusts you, don't ever betray that trust."

But as they both grew up, he was growing uncomfortable being around her so much.

These new feelings he couldn't talk about, with anyone.

On their way in, one of the other CH-53's had sustained some fatal hits and had crashed, but the men inside had all gotten out safely.

His company, Golf company, had landed on the west side of the river which divided the valley, and Hotel company, his uncle's company had landed on the east side.

Both companies had been ambushed.

The enemy had waited until most of the choppers had touched down before they opened up with mortars and small weapons, so his men had hit the ground running for cover.

They were receiving gunfire from both sides of the river and their first day had been mostly defensive.

The gunfight was now into its second day.

They had been taking a lot of sniper fire from high up on the cliffs that were on both sides of the river, and they were caught in a cross fire.

He had been calling in for artillery support and air strikes which didn't seem to be doing any good.

The enemy was dug into caves and caverns in the mountain sides, and these were too deep for any fire support to be effective.

And the triple canopy didn't help either.

Most of the artillery rounds were exploding into the tops of the trees and other vegetation. Once in a while a round would penetrate the over growth and hit the jungle floor.

The air strikes appeared to be just as useless as the artillery was so other plans had to be made to engage the enemy.

That evening he had gone with his Company Commander across the river to have a "face to face" with Hotel's Company Commander.

As they were crossing the river just before midnight, he remembered how terrified he had been.

He knew that they could be seen from above by the reflections of the moon on the calm smooth running waters of the Thu Bon River, and the ripples they were making as they struggled across the warm waters.

But as they were crossing the river, he also remembered that it was possibly the calmest he had ever been since his arrival to this beautiful yet deadly land.

"Is this how it feels just before you die?" he had thought.

Red flashing lights come on above the door and a loud buzzer on a machine by his bed was going off.

The little Hispanic nurse was astraddle of him, sitting on his chest.

Her hands were gripping his shoulders with surprising strength, and she was shaking him violently, all the while shouting.

"Wake up!"

"Don't go back to sleep!"

"Get up!"

"Don't go back to sleep!!!"

Then she was slapping him hard across the face, from right to left and back again.

Then she was pushing up and down on his ribs, as if she were trying to restart his breathing.

But he just lay there limp, taking all this punishment.

He just wanted to go home, he was so very tired.

One day he had gone into town to spend the weekend with his cousin Owen and his sister, and she was there.

Some of his aunts and uncles were up stairs playing cards and they were drinking beer while he and his cousins were in the basement playing monopoly, when she suggested they play "hide and go seek."

They were both about the same age, but she didn't look like his female cousin, who was a little older.

Instead, she was 'rounder' and she was growing into someone who was now very pleasant to look at.

Her big eyes had grown up with her as well as some of her other 'body parts', and he felt uncomfortable now when ever she would come around.

But her hair was still thin.

The young man suddenly came violently awake.

He sat up involuntarily and heaving over the side of the hospital bed, he let fly a large blood clot that had formed in his stomach.

He had been bleeding internally from the Malaria fever he was suffering with, and with this release, the nurse who had been sitting on him, was thrown to the floor.

But she stood up laughing and crying just as the doctors and other nurses burst through the door.

The man's i.v.'s were reattached and the icepacks were taken away.

After an examination and a cool sponge bath, he was allowed to go to sleep.

But the little nurse whom he had so violently pitched to the floor, insisted on staying at his bedside until all danger had passed.

He fell very quickly into a fit-full but deep sleep.

His father's younger brother was with Hotel 2/7.

When schedules allowed they visited from time to time and exchanged war stories whenever they could, or when they had a chance to drink a few beers together.

While their Captains were meeting and making their plans, his uncle had met him when they came to shore and he had introduced him as his 'cousin' to the men in his squad.

The young man had an idea that this was because the other guys in his outfit would not understand the Lakota ways, and rather than try to explain it all, this was a much easier way.

His uncle told him of the news back home and he said that his "friend" was said to be in the ranks of one of the oldest professions on earth.

"And I don't mean that she's a farmer neither!" was the way he had put it.

Everyone who heard this comment had a good laugh, but he remembered feeling very sad to hear that.

All the while he had been "in country" he had never gotten one letter from her, but he knew why.

After their short visit, he and his Captain waded back across the river and within the hour, they were scaling the almost perpendicular cliffs on their side of the river, while Hotel did the same on their side of the river.

They met no resistance on the way up the cliffs, and at dawn a thorough search of the area turned up no clues as to who the enemy was, who had been there or how many there were.

Not one casing from an expended round had been found.

Not one discarded food tin or toilet paper and not even one foot print had been found.

Everything had been picked up and all the tracks had been brushed over.

This was indeed a formidable enemy.

Not knowing who they were fighting or how many, the Marines knew they were in real danger, and they were to learn the battle was far from being over.

She had chosen him to be the first 'seeker' and he was to remain in the basement and count to 100 while the others ran outside to hide.

After the wounded and dead had been evacuated, and the company had been resupplied, the men expended their excess ammunition into the jungle.

This in itself was indeed an awesome sight to behold!

Trees and foliage that would have been hard for the men to penetrate with their machetes had been cleared away in a matter of a few minutes. Everything was cut away by the rounds being fired into the brush, even large trees were felled by the exploding rounds.

Their firepower was truly awesome.

But the young man also knew that this show of firepower was as much a warning, just in case the enemy was there watching, and he knew they were indeed up there watching.

After the men had come back down the cliffs and had regained the river bottoms, they were to start a company move up stream.

Standing on the opposite riverbank, his uncle had been waving. When he waved back, he could hear the shout, "Waonchiglaka." It was a Lakota word meaning "take care of yourself", then he disappeared into the jungle.

He had shouted back the same warning, but no one was there to hear him.

97

The young man stirred fitfully in his sleep.

Then he came awake, startled, fearful, sweating profusely, although no longer from his fever.

The little nurse applied a wet towel to his bare chest and forehead to keep him cool.

As he closed his eyes again she whispered, "Shhhhh."

"I'm here."

"You'll be fine."

"I'm here."

"I'll take care of you, I promise, there, there now, shhhhh."

When he had finished counting to one hundred and he had uncovered his eyes, she was there standing right in front of him.

The sight of her made him catch his breath.

She had put her finger to his lips to keep him quiet, then she started to undress him.

He tried to fight her at first, pushing her hands away, he was rebuttoning his shirt even as she was undoing his buttons.

Then he stopped.

Something deep inside him was stirring.

Suddenly he knew this was not the way he had imagined or had wanted it to happen.

"Not this way!!!" he had whispered in her ear.

"What's wrong?"

"Don't you want me?"

"I've been saving myself for you..."

"And you don't want me?"

"Please!!!"

"Come back!"

"Please come back, I'm sorry..."

But before he had realized it, he had climbed the stairs and he was standing outside looking around, his head was spinning.

He had left her standing there crying.

He could have handled it better.

She would have done anything he wanted.

She would have waited for him if he'd asked her...

He gave an anguished cry and the nurse came closer, whispering to him.

"Shhhhh, I'm here, I'll take care of you, I promise."

He was in the second platoon, second squad with the Captain, and second platoon was walking point.

They were followed by the first and third platoons in that order.

They had been on the trail for almost two hours when with a mighty explosion, followed by a metallic roar, the jungle came alive.

The point man had tripped a "daisy chain" and the booby trap had taken out the entire squad in front of him and the captain.

This incoming was followed immediately with intense automatic small weapons fire.

Smoke, explosions and debris filled the air.

He didn't have time for fear, but he knew anger, and anger took him over, then an overpowering rage.

Rage at the enemy!

He couldn't hear the gunfire or the screaming or the cursing, it was somehow blocked out, but he could see their faces as they fired their weapons at him and his men.

As if mechanical, he just kept reloading magazine after magazine into his M-16. And he kept firing as he moved towards the enemy, firing, reloading, firing while moving forward, reloading and firing, moving forward.

Then it was over.

There was complete silence!

It was as if everyone had run out of ammunition at the same time.

As he was reloading, he thought that everyone seemed to be holding their breath, fearing they would draw more fire if they made any noise, but he didn't care.

He had his fists clenched towards the heavens and he was cursing and shouting,

"Take me you son of a bitch, go on, take me!"

"I'm one mean son of a bitch my damn self!"

"Come on!"

"Take me!"

Then he was on his knees crying, sobbing, his chest heaving.

Great torrents of tears coming down and he was begging forgiveness for his blasphemy, praying only to be taken home safely, out of this hell, and to be allowed to live!

Then as he sat quietly weeping, he heard someone calling to him.

"Chief."

"Is that you Chief?"

"I'm over here Chief."

It was Don.

Don Manac from Fargo, Georgia.

Don Manac, the scrawny kid, the only person he had dared to make friends with.

He went to his buddy and found him lying on his back, facing up and covered with debris, seemingly untouched by all the hot metal that had just been expended.

But his buddy didn't move, so he knelt down and lit a smoke for him and put it to his lips.

Then he picked up his buddy and found his clothing and flak jacket were shredded. He could feel the blood oozing from the many wounds the booby trap had made, shredding his young body, leaving only his face and head untouched.

His buddy told him, "Chief, don't let me die like this."

"I don't want to die."

"There are so many things I haven't done yet."

"Please don't let me die like this."

All he could do was hold his friend, and try not to show emotion.

The man in the hospital bed sat bolt upright!

The nurse had to push him back down firmly as she whispered again.

"Shhhhhhhh!"

"Take it easy!"

"You're going to be alright now, sssshhhhh, I'll take care of you."

"I promise, I promise."

The young man realized he knew exactly when his uncle had been killed.

It was what had caused his anger and his blasphemy, but he also knew that he was forgiven, and that he would be allowed to live.

He also knew that he had to find his "friend" and ask her forgiveness as well.

After all, uncle Ray would have wanted it that way.

But he knew he never would.

Hau!
(for Conrad Lee)

SMOKEY

(from the author)

I took exceptional pleasure in bringing this next story to life, because my grandchildren love horses.

This story is about my grandfather, Charles William Mutchler and the great love he had for his grand children.

I hope to also show the respect he had for the animals in his care, this is something that no one shows anymore in our modern times.

Perhaps of all my grandfathers who took a hand in my up bringing, I would have to name my beloved grandpa Charlie first. But then I had many grandfathers and they each took the time to take me aside and teach me something they thought important.

Can sa (Redwood Jim) and grandpa Jerry played the next biggest parts in my young life.

I very seldom ever saw all my grandfathers gathered together at one time, only on a few occasions have I ever seen this happen.

But when they were all called together you could bet there was something very important in the works for the family.

Grandpa Jerry taught me how to throw a figure 8 when we worked calves. Then as I got older, he taught me how to cut horses even if I had to work alone.

I mention my grandpa Maynard in A DIVISION OF ARTICLES and there are some who will be introduced as these stories come to life.

In SMOKEY, a tragedy is diverted because of a young boys love and respect for his grandfather and his grandfather's horse.

So with all this in mind, grab your hat and rope, we're going to a rodeo first, then we'll see what mother nature has in store for us in SMOKEY.

SMOKEY

By
Eya Mani

When I was 10 years old, my father bought us kids each a yearling Quarter horse. Then he bought himself a beautiful black 9 year old thoroughbred mare.

My brother named his sorrel gelding Star, I named my sorrel gelding Frosty and my sister named her sorrel mare Missy.

Dad's horse was already named Pet from the previous owner, and she answered to her name so she got to keep it.

Pet was a working cattle horse. She was good at cutting cattle and she was a good roping horse as well. I liked riding her because her gait was so smooth, you could ride her all day long with or without a saddle, and not get tired.

Up until then, we used to ride grandpa's Belgian team horses.

Belgian horses are big and friendly, but their size is intimidating.

My grandfather's horses stood above 16 hands at the withers, which is over six feet tall at the shoulders.

Those big horses liked to trot and they had no rhythm, so it was bumpity bump bumpity bump.

Those bone jarring jolts could wear down the best of riders in an hour or two. But at the time, they were all we had to learn to ride on, so we learned to move with them to smooth out the ride.

It was a rough learning experience, but it was well worth it.

Then one day, a Texan came to buy some of grandpa's calves, and he brought with him a tall slim saddle horse he called Smokey.

We couldn't tell what breed Smokey was, and later when people would ask him, grandpa would say "he's a Mexican."

When grandpa got him, Smokey was already about 10 years old and they quickly formed a very close bond.

Grandpa loved and trusted old Smokey, with his life.

103

Smokey was gentle, so gentle in fact, that us kids used to ride him bare back, six back at a time.

The Texan never said anything about old Smokey being a seasoned cutting horse when it came to working cattle, but grandpa was a very good judge of 'horse flesh', and he already seemed to know what Smokey could do.

One day we were helping grandpa round up his cattle getting them together to brand his calves.

Since we were still breaking in our horses, dad thought this would be an excellent time to try and teach them to work cattle.

My horse, Frosty, learned real fast what it was we were trying to do. And after a short time he seemed to enjoy chasing these cattle around, separating the calves from their mothers and the dry cows.

We were doing pretty good on our horses, along with the other cowboys, so grandpa didn't have to saddle up old Smokey.

After we had them all separated and corralled, one of my youngest uncles showed up.

We all knew he was a show boat, and I didn't like him because he liked to treat the animals mean and take unnecessary chances with them.

While the rest of them had dinner he saddled up old Smokey without grandpa knowing about it.

All the while he was saddling up he was talking mean to him, jerking him around and punching him in the ribs.

I didn't like that, but I didn't say anything right away.

"What you know old horse?"

"You better know what to do out there Mexican."

"I don't want to be the laughing stock, you hear me?", then he'd punch old Smokey in the ribs again.

When I'd had enough, I went and told grandpa. All he did was burst out laughing and he said, "Let him go. Don't say anything to him, and don't worry. Your uncle will get his. Old Smokey ain't nothing to fool with."

"Just watch."

My uncle used to wear these spurs with really big rowels on them. Dad said they were Mexican spurs, and that they were only supposed to be worn at the rodeo, because they would cut a horse bad if the rider knew how to use them.

But I knew my uncle liked to wear these spurs because you could hear him coming from way off, jingling around like Clint Eastwood.

I think he thought it put the fear of God into the horses, but it really irritated me because he was mean and no one else ever used spurs on any of our horses.

After dinner we all went back to the corral, but instead of getting ready to brand, everyone climbed up and sat on the top railing of the corral, waiting for my uncle to bring old Smokey out of the barn and mount up.

When my uncle came out of the barn leading Smokey, he saw everyone sitting on the corral watching, so he shouted, "What's wrong with you all? C'mon let's go, we have a lot of work to do", then he mounted up.

Old Smokey didn't move. He just stood there with his ears back.

My uncle was sliding these spurs back and forth along his ribs and he was whipping him with the reins, back and forth across his rump, but Smokey just turned around and looked at my uncle sitting there on his back.

My uncle started swearing and he took off his hat and fanned him with it across the ears, then he pushed his legs out to give Smokey the full force of his spurs, that's when old Smokey cut loose.

He took a few steps back real quick, dropping down on his haunches, then he lunged high into the air, and when he hit the ground, his legs were straight.

This jolt brought my uncle off Smokey in a high arc.

He was still holding onto the reins, so this brought him down in a half circle, adding to the force of his fall.

He landed flat on his back, and he lay there unable to catch his breath.

There were 'ooohs' and 'aaahs' but no one went to help him as he struggled to his feet, gasping for breath.

If it was me, I would have stayed off, but my uncle was foolish enough, and arrogant enough, so he climbed right back on.

Smokey let him get back on and get comfortable, but he'd had enough of this guy, so he was going to dump him real good this time.

He waited again until my uncle pushed his legs out to make his move. He backed up a step or two real quick again and got down on his haunches before lunging forward. He looked like a race horse bursting out from the gates, as he streaked across the corral full out.

His neck was stretched out and he had his head down.

As Smokey was approaching the corral, my uncle shouted, "Move! We're going over!"

But Smokey came to an abrupt halt.

He stopped so suddenly that his front hoofs were digging into the soft earth and he almost went to his knees.

My uncle wasn't expecting this. He had leaned forward in anticipation of going over the corral, just as Smokey had come to a stop.

This time my uncle wisely let go of the reins.

With Smokey's speed and my uncle's quick dismount, I was surprised he had managed to clear the top railing.

I had shut my eyes, I didn't want to see this!

I was sure he would smack that top rail.

When I opened my eyes again, my uncle was sitting in a cloud of dust out and away from the corral.

When the dust cleared we could see he was facing away from the corral, slumped over forward, and I was sure he had broken his tail bone.

He had lost one of his spurs and his fancy long sleeved cowboy shirt had become untucked and it was ripped open across the back.

I didn't see it, but later they said he did a complete somersault before hitting the ground hard in the seated position I saw him in.

I think the force of his fall, tore his new fancy cowboy shirt, because we heard a loud "Uunnggh!" when he landed. It sounded like someone had squeezed the air out of him.

Someone shouted, "Wow! Did you see that?"

Someone else shouted "Hhhoolllyy shit!"

Then the expected chorus, "Reride!"

Everyone was laughing, hootin' and hollerin', except me and grandpa and grandma.

"Si si si (pronounced she she she-meaning my my my) grandma was saying as she ran past everyone and reaching her baby boy first, she tried to help him to his feet but he was angry and hurt, so he jerked away.

He had been humiliated in front of the entire family and some of his friends, by what he thought was a "stupid horse."

He was so angry he just sat there crying and he wouldn't let anyone touch him.

He slowly got to his feet and dusted himself off.

He staggered around dizzily, then he took off the remaining spur and threw it away, as far as he could.

Everyone was watching him in silence, but I don't think anyone felt bad for him...I just pitied him.

Smokey was watching him over the top railing, stomping his foot and snorting.

After he was sure that guy wouldn't be coming back, he walked over to grandpa and snorted softly, stamping his foot.

Grandpa pulled some sugar cubes out of his shirt pocket and gave them to him. Then he chuckled and said softly, "Good boy Smokey."

We didn't brand that day.

I helped grandpa unsaddle and curry comb old Smokey, then when grandpa left us alone I told him, "Smokey, you're the smartest horse I know. You're even smarter than my Frosty. Don't worry, my uncle won't bother you again, you made sure of that."

Smokey gained a lot of respect that day, from the whole family. And when the story was told of how smart he was, everyone was afraid to ride him, even some of the kids.

But I knew better.

Smokey wouldn't hurt anyone if he wasn't hurt first.

While we were combing out old Smokey, grandpa told me,

"You know, you have to respect your animals. If you take good care of them and treat them right, they will take care of you too. If you are ever lost, let him have his head, and he will bring you home. If he has too, he will die for you."

These words echoed back to me a few winters later.

One morning grandpa was up earlier than usual listening to the radio. He was drinking coffee with grandma and they were talking in hushed tones when I came into the room from the bunk house where we stayed.

He said that my father had already gone out.

There was a blizzard coming, a bad one, and we had to get the cattle back to the home place before it hit.

While I was getting dressed to go out and help my dad, grandpa was also getting dressed. On our way to the barn he told me where to go. He said that most of the cattle where already home, but there was always a few stragglers who liked to go off by themselves.

When we got to the barn, I saw that old Smokey was already saddled, so I thought he would be coming with me.

Instead, he told me to leave Frosty home, and to ride Smokey.

As I mounted up and was leaving the barn, I could hear him say, "Remember. You can trust old Smokey."

When I was riding out of sight of the home place, I could see a couple of my uncle's feeding the cattle. They were cutting the twine and throwing bales off one of the wagons pulled by grandpa's team. I knew that later, they would go back outside and give them cottonseed cake to help them through the coming cold of the blizzard.

I rode south along the White Shirt creek, and after two miles, I took the first draw south of the rocky butte, and headed east.

I hadn't seen any sign of any cattle up to this point, so after riding east a mile or so, we turned back north.

Smokey and I were out on the flat now, just above the old White Hand Bear homestead.

That's when the storm hit.

The wind came first, then small pieces of ice and snow were blowing so hard they stung my face and forced me to ride with my eyes closed and my head down.

The wind was getting stronger and we were slowly being forced more easterly until we came to the top of a large ravine.

This ravine lay more north and south but it winded back and forth east and west and it offered plenty of shelter in times of storm.

The snow had taken over now, so me and Smokey dropped into the bottom of the draw, knowing that the lost animals, if any were out here, would already be in shelter.

Riding in the bottom of the draw, I looked up and I could see the storm passing overhead. Down here in the bottom there were many small wind gusts but because of the thick forage and tree cover, only light snow was coming down.

Not seeing any sign of lost cattle here we took a short draw leading north west and back up to the flat. When we got on top we headed north again.

"I think we're in for it now Smokey" I said as Smokey took his head and he broke into a slow steady lope until we came to another deep draw. This barren draw was on the northern fringe of grandpa's land holdings.

Up to this point in our journey, I thought we might have come 5 or 6 miles and I still knew pretty much where we were. But my face was numb from the stinging blowing snow and my feet were getting numb from the cold.

From this barren draw, smaller finger draws lead out and away, north and east.

We skirted those, and not seeing any sign of livestock, we headed west toward home.

By this time I could only see a few feet ahead of us.

We were going directly into the wind, and the force of the wind and snow was fully against my face.

I couldn't keep my eyes open.

I knew Smokey's eyes must be hurting too, so I took out a bandana and tied it across the bridle, covering his eyes.

As I gave him a few cubes of sugar, I told him, "You'll have to trust me now old boy, we'll be lucky to get out of this one..."

The snow was blowing horizontally now, along with the contour of the land, and I could feel the temperature drop as the wind had increased in speed. As I remounted, I realized that we were now in a full fledged ground blizzard, and I could feel a spark of fear in the pit of my stomach.

I could at least shield my eyes and take occasional peeks from behind my hands to navigate, but old Smokey didn't have that option.

I remembered what grandpa had taught me, so Smokey and I found shelter in a deep heavily wooded draw, to wait out the storm.

I thought we might have been gone now about 4 or 5 hours and it must be around noon or maybe a little after. But the sky was getting darker so I might have been wrong. By now I was scared but I wouldn't acknowledge it at first.

I carried a bird nest with me and some wooden matches wrapped in a plastic bag, just in case, but I didn't want to use them just yet.

After an hour or so had passed, it didn't look like the storm would lift, so I said a prayer and I told Smokey, "Well, it's just you and me now boy. If we don't try we'll never know. But grandpa and grandma will be worried. We better get going."

We followed the bottom of the draw west. I knew that it would eventually lead us back to the White Shirt creek, but after what seemed a long time it never happened.

We had come down into another draw, and with the blowing snow and driving wind, I very slowly realized that I was lost, and my being scared now turned into fear.

As we continued on down the draw, I also realized I didn't know which way was north.

I didn't know where I was.

It was a complete white out now and when I looked up I could see that the clouds were breaking up, and the new brightness of the blowing snow was almost blinding.

We might have been standing in our yard, and I wouldn't have known it!

As I rode on, panic was settling in.

My feet had turned numb an hour back, and I was chilled to the bone.

Now my hands and fingers were getting numb, and I remembered grandpa's words, "Before you lose feeling in your fingers, you better start your fire. Get to shelter and start your fire."

I dismounted and walked in front of Smokey for a time. I don't know how long we wondered around, because I had now lost track of time, and I still had Smokey's eyes covered.

"My grandson, give him his head, and he will bring you home."

It was grandpa!

Somehow he had found me!

Everything would be alright now!

"Grandpa! Grandpa! I'm over here! I'm lost grandpa!"

"My grandson, give him his head and he will bring you home. We need you home. Give him his head and he will bring you home."

No.

It was my grandpa, but he hadn't found me. But now I knew what I should do.

I couldn't untie one side of the bandana, so I tucked that side around the bridle, then I tried to mount up, but I was too numb from the cold.

I couldn't lift my leg to the stirrup to mount, and I couldn't feel my fingers to grip the saddle horn.

Now I was in panic...

It was so cold the saddle leather stopped creaking, and I remembered the old ones talk of this kind of cold, and I knew I was in trouble then.

"Now I know its cold!" I tried to mumble.

"Smokey!"

I tried to shout but my lips were numb too.

But Smokey just stomped his foot in response to my plea.

I stomped around, I jumped around, and I did jumping jacks.

After awhile of looking the fool, I could feel myself warming up.

After a half hour of this, I was finally able to get back into the saddle.

Smokey whinnied and pulled on the reins, so I let him have his head.

He put his head down and we headed straight into the storm.

I hadn't realized it, but I had let the storm push us toward the south west, and from the 'feel' of it, I had somehow taken us back down to that rocky butte where we had first headed east.

Smokey kept his head down and he kept on going north along the creek bank. Dropping into the bottom once in awhile then coming back up on top.

This wasn't good because I had already started losing the feelings in my feet and hands again, and although I could see the sky above, I couldn't see in front of us at all.

After what seemed like hours, we came walking through the cattle herd and on into the open corral.

When we got close to the barn, I saw my dad and grandfather waiting by the open door.

I slid off Smokey and landed on wooden legs.

I lead Smokey in to the barn on my stiff wooden legs, tripping a few times because I still couldn't feel my feet yet.

My dad came over to ask if I was alright, then he unsaddled Smokey and took off his bridle, then he brought out the curry combs and a blanket.

But it was grandpa I wanted to see.

He was still standing by the open barn door looking out. As I got near he turned to me.

"Are you okay? How did you find your way back in this blizzard? All the cows are home. Come. Let's get inside. Your grandma's got supper waiting. You shouldn't make her worry like that. Were you lost? Were you afraid?"

"I was lost for awhile grandpa. But I remembered everything you taught me though. I almost used the bird nest too. I had to get off Smokey and jump around to get my feelings back, but I'm okay now."

"And what did you hear?"

"I heard you grandpa, you were right there with me, and I heard you. Thank you for bringing me home."

"Do you know why I wanted you to ride Smokey instead of Frost?"

"Yes grandpa, Frost is inexperienced and we would have died if I rode him. And you knew that. Thank You grandpa."

Hau!